A Gift From the Heart

Folk Tales From Bulgaria

Illustrated by Pauline Baynes

A GIFT
FROM
THE HEART

Told by Radost Pridham

THE WORLD PUBLISHING COMPANY

CLEVELAND AND NEW YORK

Published by The World Publishing Company
2231 West 110th Street, Cleveland, Ohio 44102
First American Edition 1967
Library of Congress catalog card number: 67-13819
Copyright © 1966 by Radost Pridham
Printed in the United States of America.
Designed by Eileen Billig

Contents

CONTENTS

Once Upon a Time

WHEREVER YOU GO in Bulgaria you are bound to see mountains; they dominate not only the landscape but the life of the people. Stara Planina, the Old Mountain, or the Balkan as it is always called, sprawls right across the country, cutting it into two parts, northern and southern Bulgaria. If you go north, you come upon the slow-flowing Danube. Traveling east, you reach the golden shores of the Black Sea. But the Bulgarians are not a seafaring people. They love their mountains, their green meadows, the groves of chestnut and fruit trees, the little villages ringed with poplars. Theirs is a land of rich fertility, where old peasant traditions live on and hospitality takes first place.

The Balkan Peninsula has been invaded many times. When the Bulgar warrior tribes from the east conquered the peaceful Slav inhabitants in the seventh century, they gave their name to the country known since as Bulgaria.

The peasants have always believed that they were surrounded by supernatural enemies, against whom they must be on their guard. All sorts of demons, vampires, serpents, spirits of fountains, and a great variety of fairies have survived until today in the folk tales and songs of Bulgaria. Christianity dispelled some of the peasants' fears, but not all. They believed that only the eagle could fly high enough to reach and talk to God.

For many centuries past, the Bulgarian peasant owned land and kept sheep, oxen, goats, cows, sturdy little horses, and overworked donkeys. He shared his life and his home with the animals. As often as not the flocks were looked after by the children who not only knew a great many stories about wolves and bears, but sometimes had to learn from experience how to outwit poisonous snakes and thieving foxes.

In summer the Bulgarian shepherds would leave their wives and children and take large herds high up in the mountains to greener pastures. In the mountains the grassy meadows looked as if no human being had ever trod there before. The lakes were so crystal clear that one could see the trout playing. Among the pine tops a magpie would give a warning cry to the animal kingdom on the approach of men. And today you can still hear the mountain shepherd playing on his pipes.

If you ask a peasant whether he believes in fairies, he will slowly nod his head in a way which means "yes" to us but "no" to the Bulgarians. But in the old folk tales bad fairies inhabited the highest mountain peaks, or lived in lakes and forests, often bringing whirlwinds and storms and hailstones as big as birds' eggs. Sometimes a young man would fall in love with one of the fairies, for they were "beautiful beyond words, bathed in dew, dressed in wild flowers, and living on milk," as the Bulgarian folk song says.

There were good fairies as well as bad, and they lived in trees and in mountain springs whose water was delicious to drink and could often cure illnesses. In gratitude the peasants built stone fountains, some of which are still standing.

Not all the folk tales are about fairies. A great many of them tell simply of the everyday life of the Bulgarians. They reflect their humor and acceptance of the hard realities of life.

Some of the old customs, folk tales, songs, and dances seem to live forever. They are like the Bulgarian chain dance, the horo, a solid link between a distant past and a fast-changing present. Today the Bulgarian people no longer have their Czars, voyvodas—military chieftains— and boyars—big landowners. But they still cherish their national heritage, and Bulgarian children are brought up with the stories in this book.

The folk tales were first collected by the Bulgarian writer Angel Karalyichev, and have since been translated into most European languages as part of common European folklore.

A Gift From the Heart

ONCE UPON A TIME three brothers set off for foreign lands to make their fortunes. They had not gone far when they came to a crossroads.

"Let us separate here," said the eldest. "I'll turn right; you," he told the second brother, "go left; and you," he ordered the youngest, "keep straight on. In three years' time, on St. Demetrius' day, we will meet again here at the crossroads, and then we shall see how each of us has fared. Do you agree?"

"Yes, let us do that," said the two younger brothers. They kissed the hand of the eldest and took their leave.

The eldest brother went to a town and became a baker. By the end of three years he had saved a bagful of golden coins.

The second brother opened a tavern close to a bridge. Selling mostly wine and water, he made a tidy sum of money, and at the end of the time his pockets were full.

The youngest took service with a good master—an old shepherd. When three years had passed, he went to ask for his wages. The shepherd counted out the money and

gathered it into a small heap. Then he took three walnuts out of the sash round his waist.

"I am old and weak, and I can't run after the sheep
now as I used to," he said. "It's a good thing I found
you, for otherwise I should have lost all my sheep. I am
most grateful to you for looking after my flock. All this
money in front of you is what is due to you, but I have
also saved these three walnuts. The money is not from
my heart, because money is like fire—it is easy to burn
your fingers with it. But the walnuts are another matter:
those I give you from my heart. You can take the money,
or you can take the walnuts, whichever you like; but you
can't have both."

The young man thought for a while, thought again,
then reached out for the walnuts.

"I'll take the walnuts, because they are from the
heart," he said.

And he put them in his pocket, kissed the old shepherd's hand, and left him.

At the crossroads, on St. Demetrius' day, the three
brothers met.

"Have you done well?" asked the eldest.

"Not badly," said the second.

"Let's see. But first I'll show you what I have made!"
And so saying the eldest brother pulled out a purse full
of gold coins.

"You have done well, but my purse is just as full as
yours," said the second brother, and he took out his own
fat purse.

Then the youngest brother put his hand into his pocket and fished out the three walnuts.

"Is that all you have earned for three years' work?" cried his brothers.

"Yes—only three walnuts, but given to me from the heart," said the boy. "An old man, a shepherd, gave them to me for looking after his sheep. But he looked after me like a real father."

The other two lost their tempers.

"We've seen simple people before, but never a greater fool than you!" shouted the eldest brother. "Where else in the whole wide world could you find anybody ready to work three years for nothing! Go straight back to the old shepherd and ask him for the money, and don't you dare come home again without it!"

The boy was saddened. He went slowly back, his heart heavy.

"And I thought," he said to himself, "that a gift from the heart was the best thing in this world, and now look what has happened!"

Coming to a fountain, he bent down to drink some water. But all he could swallow was two gulps, because he was so hungry. He looked in his bag. There was not even a crumb of bread.

"I'd better crack the walnuts—they will stay my hunger for a while," he thought.

He took out one of the walnuts and cracked it on a stone; but to his amazement, instead of splitting open, the nut began to swell. Larger and larger it grew, till it

was bigger than the biggest barrel the young man had ever seen. Then it burst open, and out streamed a whole flock of fat sheep—ewes, frolicking lambs, and rams with bells jingling at their necks.

The young man was beside himself with joy. Rounding up the sheep, he set off for his father's house.

As he drew near the village he said to himself, "I'd better crack the second walnut and see if there is anything in that."

And he took out another walnut and cracked it on a stone. The walnut swelled and swelled. At last it burst open, and out of it came clopping two young bullocks with long horns. Behind them was a cart, and on the cart was an iron plow.

"Well, I never!" cried the young man in astonishment. And he took hold of the head chain and led the bullocks after the flock of sheep.

Just before he entered the village he stopped again. "I'll just see what's inside the third walnut," he said to himself, and he cracked it open.

Out stepped a young girl, beautiful beyond words.

"Lead me to your father's house," she said. "I am to be your wife."

Joyfully the young man helped the girl onto the cart. He shouted to the bullocks and they started forward, the bells of the sheep ringing behind them so that all the village heard and came running out to see who was coming. And when he brought the girl to his father's house there was dancing and merrymaking and a wedding with guests from nine villages.

The Magic Pipe

THERE WAS ONCE a young shepherd boy who, like all Bulgarian shepherds in the mountains, had a pipe on which he played all day long. His pipe was carved from wood and looked simple enough, but the music it made was as sweet as honey. As soon as the lad put it to his lips, all the sheep would stand stock-still, as if rooted to the spot. Then, as the young shepherd played, they and every other living creature around would begin to dance. And what a dance it was! They simply could not stop.

One morning, as the boy was putting some bread into his knapsack before going off for the day, the old man who owned the sheep said to him, "Let me give you some good advice. Play a little less music on your pipe, and pay a little more attention to my sheep!"

But when the young shepherd came back in the evening, driving the flock in front of him, the old man took one look at him and said angrily, "What are you up to? Where did you take my flock? Why didn't you look after my sheep properly? Just look at the state they are in! They look as if they'll drop dead any moment from sheer hunger!"

"But I do look after them, Grandfather, I tell you, I do!" replied the boy. "I take them to the nicest places I know. I even cut juicy green branches for them to eat."

It was the same the next day, and the day after. The old man was certain that the young shepherd would be the death of his sheep.

At last the old man decided to see for himself what was happening. He got up very early one day and quietly followed the unsuspecting boy into the forest. There he hid himself in a thick bush of sweetbrier from which he could watch the sheep. He saw the lad take them into a clearing and cut some leafy branches. The old man could hear the sheep munching them.

Then the boy, remembering his music, took his pipe out of his red sash and put it to his lips. The sheep stopped chewing at once, and raised their heads to listen. Then, all together, they began to dance. And the old man in the bush found that he must dance too. His old knee lifted, and hop! hop! hop! he joined in the merry dance. His clothes were torn to shreds in the sweetbrier, but he could not stop.

"Boy, stop it!" he shouted. "Don't play any more! The thorns are tearing my clothes to rags."

"I wish I could stop, Grandfather, but it's not me, it's the pipe that doesn't want to."

And Grandfather danced, and the sheep danced too, quite unable to stop.

Meanwhile the old man's wife was waiting for him at home. At last she lost patience and said to herself, "I will go and see what Grandfather is doing."

Off she went to the forest, and there she saw the shepherd playing his pipe and the sheep jigging and prancing round him. At last she caught sight of her old husband stamping around, hop! hop! hop! in the sweetbrier.

"Shepherd! Hey! Grandfather! What are you doing there?" she cried. But the pipe was playing even louder than before, and in no time hop! hop! hop! the old woman was in full swing too.

Now this old couple had a son and daughter-in-law with children of their own, and being a true Bulgarian family they all lived together under the same roof. The son, who had been waiting at home for the return of his old parents, could wait at last no longer.

"Something must have happened to my mother and father," he said to his wife. "You wait here, wife, while I go and see where they are."

He set off toward the forest. In the distance he could hear the pipe playing. Then he saw the sheep bouncing about, and his mother and father dancing as if they had lost all control of their old legs.

"Whatever are you up to, my dears?" he called out.

But the pipe was playing more joyfully than ever and soon the son joined in the dance too.

The daughter-in-law, at home with the children, waited for a long time. Nobody seemed to want to come home that day. She wondered what they could all be doing.

"I must go and see for myself," she decided in the end. So she left the children to look after themselves and went into the forest. And there she saw the shepherd playing his pipe, and the sheep, her own husband, and his old parents all dancing like mad.

"My dears, what is the matter? What are you celebrating?" she called out to them.

Nobody had enough breath left to answer her. And before long—hop! hop! hop! she was dancing too.

In the meantime the children had become curious to know where their parents had gone. They ran to the forest, and seeing the whole family dancing, and the sheep as well, they laughed and shouted.

"Let's dance, let's all dance together! Faster, faster, shepherd!" they cried.

And they began capering about, hop! hop! hop! too.

All day long the merry dance went on. The boy played, and the sheep danced, and the whole family danced with them. Night came, and they all set off for home. First went the shepherd, still playing his magic pipe, with the sheep skipping after him. Behind them, still jigging and jumping, came the grandfather, the grandmother, the son, the daughter-in-law, and all the children. And as they passed through the village everyone who saw them joined in the dance, hop! hop! hop!—until at last the whole village was dancing in a long chain.

They danced all night and maybe they are dancing still.

Simple and the Princess

THERE WAS ONCE a Czar who had to buy his daughter a new pair of shoes every day. Each morning the pair he had given her the day before was quite worn out. To the Czar this seemed very strange; he could not imagine what his daughter did to wear out her shoes so quickly.

"Perhaps she goes out somewhere every night," he thought. And he decided to have her followed.

All through the kingdom went a proclamation saying that the Czar would give his daughter in marriage to the man who could discover where she went each night, and that anyone who tried to follow her and failed would have his head cut off.

Many brave young men tried their luck. The first one lay down outside the Princess' door, but he was soon overcome with sleep and could tell the Czar nothing the next day. Twenty-eight others watched at the Princess' door, one after another, but each one fell asleep before he could discover how the Princess wore out her shoes.

On the very day on which the twenty-nine young men

were to be beheaded, another young man, whose name was Simple because he was only a simpleton, came to the palace and presented himself to the Czar.

"Your Majesty," said he, "what will you give me if I can find out where your daughter goes each night, and what she does there, and why she wears out her shoes?"

"You shall become my son-in-law, and half my kingdom will be yours," declared the Czar. "But if you follow her and fail, you'll lose your head like all the others."

"Then I shall try my luck tonight," said Simple. And off he went to prepare himself.

He arrived back at the palace that evening earlier than the others had done, and he was dressed for a long journey. He lay down in front of the Princess' door and closed his eyes. He was soon snoring loudly.

When the pretty Princess saw him she laughed.

"Silly Simple, fancy thinking you can watch over me!" she said. "So soon asleep and snoring already! What will happen later tonight? Braver men than you have tried to find out my secret and failed. And you imagine you are cleverer than I am!"

Simple was not really asleep, of course, but only pretending. Hearing how the Princess mocked him, he said to himself, "Well, we shall see who is going to be surprised!"

And so the Princess went into her room, and soon Simple really did fall asleep.

In the middle of the night he was awakened by a rushing sound, like wind. He saw a huge, glittering shape before him—a great dragon, with scales so bright that they lit up the whole chamber.

Simple lay still, watching through half-closed eyes as the dragon knocked very softly on the Princess' door with his great claw. A minute later the door opened a crack and the Princess slipped out, wearing a beautiful dress and a new pair of shoes. She greeted the dragon and the two of them hurried down the stairs and out of the palace.

As soon as their backs were turned Simple jumped to his feet and set out after them, keeping at a safe distance. From the Czar's palace he followed them into the great park. As they walked along, the dragon took out a posy of golden flowers and tossed it to the Princess, his sweetheart. She caught the posy and threw it back to him, and they went on their way playing and laughing.

Simple had hurried ahead and was hiding behind the trunk of a big tree. As the Princess and the dragon passed by, playing their game, the posy of golden flowers fell by the side of the tree where Simple stood. He picked it up and put it in his pocket. The Princess looked around to see where it had fallen.

"I threw the flowers to you. Don't go and hide them!" cried the dragon. "Are you trying to deceive me?"

"I didn't see you throwing them to me," replied the Princess. "You must still have them yourself. You can see my hands are empty."

The dragon didn't feel like arguing. "Well, never mind, let's go on," he said.

And away they went. But before Simple left the tree, he chopped out a little piece of the bark with his hatchet, as proof for the Czar that he had followed the Princess.

The Princess heard the noise and asked the dragon, "Who could be chopping trees in the middle of the night?"

"Don't be afraid, my love," said the dragon. "There is nobody here. Let's go on."

And so they continued on their way. Soon they came to a river flowing under a stone bridge. Simple slid under the bridge and knocked off a little piece as another proof for the Czar. The young Princess stopped.

"Don't tell me you can't hear *that!*" she said. "Someone must be following us."

"Bah! What does it matter?" said the dragon. "Let him knock, whoever he is. Who cares? You have nothing to fear, my love."

And so they went on until they came to yet another river, much larger than the first, and with no bridge across it. The dragon lifted the Princess in his arms and flew over the water. It was not so easy for Simple.

The river was wide and deep, and Simple thought it was a waste of time looking for a shallow place to wade across. He followed the bank in search of a bridge, but no bridge was to be found. To make matters worse, he could hardly see where he was going. So far his way had been lit by the dragon, but now the dragon was so far ahead that Simple could not see so much as the glimmer of his tail.

As he was wandering about he heard angry voices, and through the darkness he made out two crabbed figures, arguing fiercely together. Between them lay a frying pan made of leather, a lambskin cap, and a little silver stick. They were not human beings (though Simple did not know this) but demons who had taken human form for a while.

"Now, my fine fellows, what are you quarreling about? Can't you be friends?" asked Simple.

"We can't divide what we have here, and nobody can help us," said the demons. And, both at once, they tried to tell Simple what had happened. One of them insisted that the frying pan, the cap, and the silver stick had been left to him by his father, and the other swore that they came to him from his grandfather. And neither was prepared to hand the things over to the other.

"Are they so necessary that you can't do without them?" asked Simple. "What are they for?"

"What are they for!" exclaimed both demons at once. "With them we can cross any river without getting wet!"

It struck Simple as odd that this was precisely what he wanted to do himself. So he asked the two strangers how they could achieve such an impossible feat.

"You see this frying pan?" said one of them. "All you have to do is to sit down in it and give it a tap with the silver stick, and in less than the flicker of an eyelid you'll be across the river. And if you put the cap on, you will become invisible."

Simple saw how lucky he was to have met these two. He assured them that he knew how to settle their quarrel, and asked them to hand over their inheritance so that he could divide it fairly.

No sooner had the demons given him their precious possessions than Simple jumped into the frying pan, tapped it lightly with the silver stick, gaily put the cap of lambskin on his head, and in less than the flicker of an eyelid found himself on the other side of the river. He kept the magic charms in case they would come in useful.

Meanwhile the dragon and the Princess had covered the greater part of their journey. Simple was close enough now to see the dragon glimmering like a glowworm in the darkness. When the two lovers at last reached the dragon's palace and went in, Simple put on the lambskin cap so that he became invisible and sneaked without trouble through the half-opened door. The Princess and the dragon were resting in a large room. Simple stayed with them and watched.

Soon the Princess was tired of resting and wanted to play again. The dragon took out of his sash a golden apple and threw it to his sweetheart. The Princess caught it and threw it back, and so they played for a while. Suddenly the Princess dropped the golden apple. It rolled close to where Simple stood, so he snatched it up and put it in his pocket. The two lovers searched for it and began to argue again.

"I threw the golden apple to you. Where have you hidden it?" asked the dragon crossly.

"I am sure you've got it," said the Princess. "You are teasing me!"

But there was no trace of the golden apple anywhere.

"It is time for me to return home," announced the Princess at last. "Very soon the cocks will start crowing."

"Yes, let's go," agreed the dragon.

And off they went, with Simple hurrying after. The dragon crossed the river with one jump and this time Simple did the same, thanks to his frying pan. When they came to the second river, he ran ahead of the Princess and the dragon. He wanted to be found asleep in front of the Princess' door.

He lay down just as the dragon and the Princess came in. They saw him asleep where they had left him. The dragon took leave of his sweetheart, and the Princess went straight to bed and fell asleep.

The next morning the Czar went to examine his daughter's shoes and found them, as usual, completely worn out.

"Now, my daughter, where did you go last night?" said he. "Look at your shoes!"

"I have not been anywhere, Papa," lied the Princess.

"Well, we'll call the simpleton I left to guard you, my dear. Perhaps we can learn something about your night's adventures from him."

"Oh, yes, do that!" cried the Princess, laughing.

So Simple was brought before the Czar and his daughter.

"Now then, Simple, tell me," said the Czar. "Did you keep watch over my daughter last night?"

"I followed her, Your Majesty."

At these words the young Princess jumped up.

"How dare you say you followed me, you silly boy, when I know you didn't!" she said, stamping her foot. "Speak! We'll soon see if you're telling the truth."

Simple bowed.

"Your Highness, I will tell everything I know," he said.

And to the astonishment of the Czar and his daughter he did indeed tell the whole story from beginning to end. And he took out the bark, the piece of stone from the bridge, and the posy of golden flowers to show the Czar. Last of all, he handed him the golden apple. Then he turned to the Princess.

"Have I told the truth, Your Highness?" he asked.

The Princess blushed with shame and admitted to her father that everything Simple had said was true. So the Czar fulfilled his promise and gave Simple half of his kingdom and the Princess for a wife.

And as for the dragon, he was never seen again.

The Unwashed Pot

ALTHOUGH GRANDFATHER PETKO and Grandmother Penna had lived a long time, their life together was not very easy because they did not help each other.

One day Grandmother Penna cooked some bean soup. When it was ready the two old people noisily ate up all that was in their plates, and beamed with contentment.

Then Grandmother Penna said, "I cooked the soup. Now it's your turn to get busy and wash up the pot. I'll be needing it tomorrow when I milk the cow."

"I can't do woman's work!" said Grandfather Petko. "You must wash it yourself."

"I will not wash it!"

"Then leave it unwashed."

Night came. The two old people went to bed, the pot still unwashed.

"Listen!" said Grandfather Petko. "You must get up early tomorrow and boil some milk. I am going to the forest, and I want bread and milk for breakfast."

"How can I milk the cow when the pot is not clean?"

said Grandmother Penna. "If you wash it, I'll milk the cow into it."

"I'm not going to wash it," said Grandfather Petko.

They lay in silence for a while. Then Grandfather Petko said, "Well, let's see who can hold out the longest."

"Yes, let's!" agreed Grandmother Penna. "What shall we do?"

"We'll both keep silent, and whoever speaks first must wash the pot."

They stopped talking and soon fell asleep. The night rolled over and the sun appeared. All the peasants went to work. The village herdsman rounded up the cattle and led them to the meadow to graze. But the old couple's cow was left mooing in the yard, for there was nobody to milk her and take her to the herdsman.

The two old people sat and sat, saying nothing. The neighbors looked over the fence to see what was happening in Grandfather Petko's house, why the cow was still tied up and bellowing, and why there was no sign of life in the courtyard. They came into the house.

"What is the matter, Grandmother Penna? Why don't you milk the cow?"

Grandmother Penna kept quiet. She did not utter a word.

"Grandfather Petko, say something! Why is Grandmother Penna silent?"

But Grandfather Petko only shook his head like a horse.

"Good gracious!" exclaimed one of the neighbors at last. "These poor old people have lost their voices. Quick, call the doctor! Ignat, my boy, run along and tell the doctor to come at once!"

Little Ignat ran for the doctor, who lived at the other end of the village, up the hill. While he was gone the neighbors began to drift away. One was in a hurry to get to his field, another wanted to go to market, a third had work to do at home. Only two people stayed with the dumb couple—the priest and an old woman.

At last the priest also got up to go.

"You stay here, my dear, and look after the old people. See that nothing happens to them until the doctor arrives," he said to the old woman.

"Oh, I can't do that, Father!" said the old woman. "I can only stay if you pay me. Nobody does anything nowadays without being paid."

"Pay you? Where have you ever seen a priest paying?" said the priest.

Looking around him he noticed a ragged jerkin hanging on the wall.

He reached up and took the jerkin down.

Grandmother Penna jumped to her feet and shouted, "If you give my jerkin to that lazy woman, what do you think I'm going to wear myself?"

When Grandfather Petko heard his wife's words, he got up and rubbed his hands with glee. "There you are, Grandmother!" he said. "It was you who spoke first and you've lost. Get busy and do what you have to do!"

So Grandmother Penna, muttering crossly to herself, stumped off to wash the pot.

The Spring of Youth

IN BULGARIA PEOPLE grow to a greater age than anywhere in the world, and the older they grow the longer
they want to stay alive. And so, once upon a time, a
Czar who was nearing a hundred called his three sons
to him to send them on a journey.

"I hear that in some faraway country there is a spring
whose water bestows eternal youth," he said. "If a young
man drinks it he does not grow old, if an old man like
myself drinks it he grows young again, and if a sick man
drinks it he is cured. I will happily give up my throne
if I can taste this miraculous water, and I have decided
that whichever of you brings me some shall become
Czar."

Now the eldest son was already married and had grow-
ing children. The middle one was betrothed, and the
youngest was still free. But all of them had to leave home
and set off at once in search of the water of eternal
youth.

Before long they came to a crossroads. There stood a
drinking fountain of white marble, on which were en-
graved these words:

"Traveler, take heed. He who takes the road to the left will return safe and well. He who takes the middle road may come back, or he may not come back. And he who takes the road to the right will certainly perish."

The Czar's sons hesitated.

"What shall we do now?" asked the eldest.

"Which road should we take if we are to find the water?" said the second.

"Don't trouble your heads over that, brothers," said the youngest. He turned to his eldest brother. "You, as the eldest, with a wife and children, must take the left-hand road and come back safe and sound. You," he said to the other, "you have a young betrothed who will be waiting for you, so you must take the middle road. You have promised to make her happy, so you must take care of yourself.

"As for me, I will take the road from which it says there is no return. I am neither married nor engaged, and nobody will weep for me if I fail to come back. If you both agree to this, let us each leave a ring under this slab of marble. When one of us returns and takes up his ring, he will know who has come back and who has not."

And so the three brothers set forth, each following a different road.

The youngest, after he had walked a long way, came to a cave. A heap of straw was burning at the entrance, and from the depths of the cave came a plaintive call for help.

"Brave young man, be a brother to me and save me and my children," said the voice. "Every time we have tried to crawl out, the flames have driven us back."

The young prince beat down the flames with his sword and strode into the cave. Something was glimmering in the dark, and when he stepped nearer he saw that it was a serpent with her little ones. The young man picked them up and carried them all to safety.

"You are not only brave but kind," said the mother serpent. "Tell me, what can I do for you?"

"If you knew, you could tell me where to find the spring of youth," said the young man.

The serpent drew a small silver ring from her tail.

"Take this ring," she said, "and travel on toward the east, until you come to a high mountain. At the top you will find a silver palace. That is where my brother lives. From his palace he can see everything that happens, far beyond the mountains and rivers. If you give him my silver ring he will direct you to the spring."

So the young prince walked on, always to the east, and at last reached the silver palace on top of the mountain. But he could not see a living soul anywhere.

In front of the palace flowed a strange river, full of silvery water. As the prince approached it he saw a little golden fish jump out of the water and fall on the river bank, where it squirmed and leaped about, trying vainly to reach the river again. The prince, pitying its plight, picked it up and threw it back into the water. At once there was a blinding flash which lit up the palace and revealed a winged dragon in the doorway.

"What do you want, young man?" thundered the dragon.

The prince handed him the silver ring, saying, "I am searching for the spring of eternal youth. Can you tell me where to find it?"

"Keep walking eastward," said the dragon, "and you will come to a palace made of precious stones. There lives a damsel, queen of that kingdom, who has no equal in beauty in all the world." He took a diamond from under his wing and handed it to the prince. "If you give her this she will tell you where to find the water of eternal youth."

Once more the young prince set out eastward. When he came to the palace made of precious stones, he saw a golden eagle lying helpless on the ground with outstretched wings and open beak. The prince bent down to take the eagle in his arms, and poured a few drops of water into its mouth. The bird revived and flew away, and the young prince entered the palace.

The first person he saw was a young maiden lying asleep. She was of an almost blinding beauty, and dazzled the prince's eyes so that he had to blink hard. But he was not dreaming, for the lovely girl woke up, and he handed her the diamond. She smiled at him, and asked him what his errand was.

"I am searching for the spring of eternal youth," replied the young man.

"You have come far, and now you are very near it," she said. "Take this golden ring and put in on your left hand. Draw some water from the spring you will find outside in the garden. With the ring you will return safe and sound to the place you came from; and if you find yourself in trouble, just put it on your right hand, and everything you wish will come true."

The prince was filled with joy. He took the ring, thanked the beautiful maiden, and went out to fill a silver flask with the water of eternal youth.

After he had turned for home and gone on his way a little while, he remembered the ring. Transferring it from his left to his right hand, he said, "Little ring, please take me quickly to the fountain by the crossroads."

Hardly had he spoken the words when a terrible storm blew up and the prince found himself standing at the crossroads. He looked under the marble slab to see if his brothers were back, but their rings were where they had left them. Again the prince spoke to the ring.

"Little ring, please bring my brothers here to me."

And they both appeared almost at once.

"Where have you been, brothers?" asked the youngest.

"I was held captive in a foreign kingdom," said the eldest, "but a silver dragon with a tail of pure gold found me, and I flew here on his back."

"I was lost in a big pine forest," said the second brother, "but a dragon, also with a golden tail, came flying toward me, and he brought me here."

"And I found the spring of youth in a strange land, guarded by a queen, the most beautiful maiden in the world," said the youngest prince. "It was she who gave me this ring. All I need to do is to put it from my left to my right hand and all my wishes are fulfilled at once. Now, let us return to the palace and present the water of eternal youth to our father!" And so they set forth.

After a while the eldest brother said, "I was thinking about the ring and wondering if it would obey me, too?"

The young prince took off his ring and handed it to his brother readily. The brother thrust it on to his own right hand and said, "I want to possess the flask of water of eternal youth and I wish my youngest brother to take the road of no return once more."

The young prince stood petrified. He did not even notice when his brothers took the silver flask from him, nor did he seem to realize that he had turned back and was already walking away. Slowly he recovered his spirits, but he was still on the fateful road of no return.

Meanwhile the two brothers were back in their father's palace. The eldest presented him with the flask of miraculous water, and in return was given the throne. He demanded from the ring that his brother should become the Czar of a neighboring state. Indeed, the little ring rendered him countless services.

One day the new Czar remembered the beautiful maiden his youngest brother had spoken of. Thinking he would like to have a look at her, he changed the ring from his left to his right hand and said, "I want the queen-keeper of the water of eternal youth to present herself here!"

A magnificent golden carriage appeared in front of the

palace and out stepped the beautiful maiden, queen-keeper of the spring of eternal youth. She bowed to the Czar.

"What do you want from me, Your Majesty?" she asked.

The Czar smiled. "I want you to stay here with me, in my palace," he said.

"So it shall be. As long as the ring is on your finger, I am in your power. But I warn you that deep in your heart you will not know what joy is until your brave young brother has returned."

By this time the young prince had again reached the cave where he had once saved the serpent and her family. The young serpents came out to greet him, and he noticed that their mother was missing.

"Where is the old serpent?" he asked.

"She died of grief when she learned that the magic ring was no longer in your hands," said one of the young serpents. "But we believe that you will find it one day."

When the prince reached the silver palace, he saw that the big doors were closed. But suddenly he heard a voice coming from the silvery river.

"Do you want to see the dragon?"

"Yes," said the prince. "Where is he?"

"He died of sorrow when he learned that the ring had come into unworthy hands. But you must go on to the palace of precious stones."

So the young prince went on, and when he entered the glittering palace, how empty it looked to him! The golden eagle—the one he had once revived with a few drops of water—alighted on a window sill, and asked him why he had come all the way back again.

"I want to see the young mistress of this palace," said the prince.

"But she lost her kingdom, brave young man," said the eagle. "She is now your eldest brother's captive. And for as long as he has the ring, she will be in his power."

The prince broke down and cried bitterly. So everything was lost! The eagle perched on his shoulder and said, "Don't despair! I'll try to recover the ring for you. You just wait here. I shan't be long."

"I wish you good luck, my friend," said the prince.

And while the young prince sat waiting in the palace, the golden eagle flew swiftly to his brother, the Czar, who was walking in his garden. The eagle swooped down like a falling arrow, nipped the Czar's right hand with its beak, and soared up into the sky again. The courtiers ran to help, and the royal physician came hurrying with balms to dress the wound. But before the Czar reached his bedchamber, his hand had already begun to swell.

"Oh!" he moaned. "I'm dying! Take off this ring—the pain is too much to endure! Leave it on the table next to my bed, and call two guards to keep watch over it! And open wide the windows. Quickly! I need air!"

There was a rush to carry out the Czar's orders. The moment the windows were opened, the golden eagle flew into the bedchamber, snatched up the ring in its beak, and flew out again. The court was thrown into confusion.

The eagle was soon back with the young prince, and gave him the ring. The prince thanked him and lost no time in wishing himself back in his brother's palace.

When he reached the palace his eldest brother threw himself at his feet, sobbing with remorse.

"Brother!" he cried. "I deserve the severest punishment you can give!"

The courtiers crowded around, and the old father hurried up and embraced his youngest son joyfully. In his retirement he had no cares of state to trouble him, and he was feeling very sprightly. Then the beautiful captive queen approached the prince. She greeted him with a kiss, and turned to the old man.

"It is your youngest son who found the spring of eternal youth for you," she said. "He is so good and brave that he deserves to reign after you."

"Then reign after me he shall!" said the old man. He gave a wise smile. "I was foolish to seek the cure for old age so far away," he said. "There is youth and beauty and happiness here, and I bless them in both of you and wish nothing more for myself."

So the youngest son became Czar and married the beautiful girl, and together they ruled wisely and well over their people. As for the eldest son, he was forgiven, and returned in peace to his wife and children.

The Uninvited Guest

SO MANY STORIES were told about Sly Peter that a certain peasant decided that he must go and see for himself what sort of man he really was. No peasant in Bulgaria ever believes all he hears. He will smile under his mustache, shake his head, and say, "Is that so, indeed?" —but he is seldom taken in.

This curious peasant wanted to invite himself to Sly Peter's house, and as he could not possibly call at a stranger's house with empty hands he took a very old hen as a present. Peter thanked him politely for the gift and asked him to stay for supper. They ate and drank well, and the peasant went back to his village well satisfied with the visit.

Not long afterward he decided to go and see Sly Peter again. He knocked at the door.

"Who's there?" called Sly Peter.

"The one who brought you the hen."

"Well, well!" said Sly Peter, opening the door. "As you have come just at suppertime, you had better stay and eat with us. Come in and make yourself at home."

The peasant did not wait to be asked a second time. He sat down and ate as much as he could.

A few days later, another peasant arrived at Sly Peter's door and announced that he was a cousin of the one who had given Peter a hen for a present.

"Well!" said Sly Peter. "Every guest is an honor to me and my house, Please sit down. I hope you will stay for supper."

The following day a third peasant paid an unexpected visit. He said that he too was a cousin of the one who had given Peter a hen for a present.

"Is that so?" cried Sly Peter. "Well, I never! Another cousin, eh? Well, well, come in and sit down!"

When suppertime came, Sly Peter put a soup tureen of hot water on the table and invited the peasant to have some. When they had finished, Sly Peter turned to his guest.

"Well, my friend, how did you like the soup? Was it to your taste? Perhaps you didn't like it? And yet this soup was from the same pot in which my wife boiled the old hen your cousin brought me for a present!"

They say in the country that peasants have no shame. But this one did not know where to look until Sly Peter relieved his embarrassment by roaring with laughter.

The Spoiled Daughter

A HUSBAND AND WIFE lived in a village with their only daughter, who was called Galinka. They loved her so much that they could scarcely bear a speck of dust to fall on her. When she was small they were always carrying her in their arms to save her walking. They would never let her do anything for herself.

Every morning Galinka would lie in her bed until late. When she grew tired of her bed, her mother would dress her, comb her hair, and feed her, just like a baby, spooning the food into Galinka's mouth. Then she would spread a soft rug for her daughter to lie on, leave her something nice to eat, and go out to work.

All the neighbors said Galinka was spoiled, because when she grew up she still did nothing, nothing at all, all day long, while her father and mother worked hard to give her food and clothes. When the time came for Galinka to get married, many suitors came to see her, but they all went away again.

"No, this is not the wife for a poor, hard-working fellow like me," said each one to himself, and he would look for a wife elsewhere.

One day an old couple arrived with their only son, who liked Galinka very much and seemed to think that she was just the wife for him. Galinka's mother was quite willing to give her daughter away in marriage, but she had plenty to say to the young man's parents first.

"My sweet little girl is not used to work, and she must not get tired," she said. "She must be well looked after. Don't make her sweep the house and the yard with a broom or the dust will get into her eyes. Don't send her to the well for water; her shoulders are frail and she is not used to carrying heavy things. And mind you don't forget to put a pillow of down feathers under her head. Galinka always sleeps on something soft."

The two old people looked at each other, but said nothing.

"And promise me you will never reproach Galinka," the mother went on. "Her ears are not used to harsh words."

"Don't worry, there are no harsh words in our house," said the bridegroom's father. He got into his cart. His wife settled herself down beside him, and the bridegroom and his bride sat down behind.

The journey was a long one, for the village where they lived was tucked far away in the Valley of Roses. But as soon as they arrived that night, the mother rolled up her sleeves briskly and set to work to make a large cheese pastry. She killed a young chicken and boiled it in a saucepan. Then she went down to the cellar to draw some wine.

While all this was going on, Galinka just sat on a wooden stool with her hands crossed in her lap, thinking to herself, "What a good housewife my mother-in-law is! Just like my mother! It will be nice living here."

They all had a good supper and went to bed.

The next morning the old father woke up very early and roused the household.

"Come on, everybody, time to get up!" he shouted. "The sooner we start for the fields, the better!"

"What are we going to do there?" asked Galinka, rubbing her sleepy eyes.

"We are going to hoe the maize," said her father-in-law.

"With hoes?" asked the young bride.

"Why, yes, with hoes, of course! What else?" said her mother-in-law.

"Then I am not coming."

"Not coming? Why not? asked her bridegroom.

"Oh, because a hoe is much too heavy for me!" said Galinka.

"Leave her alone!" said the old father. "Let her tidy up the house and get the supper ready tonight. It's just as well to leave somebody in the house."

The three of them went off to the fields, leaving the young bride behind. It was noon before Galinka got out of bed, and then she got up only because she felt hungry.

She searched everywhere for something to eat, but there was nothing to be found.

"They left me nothing to eat at all! They have forgotten all about me!" thought Galinka with surprise. And just to stretch her legs, she strolled into the garden to have a look at the flowers.

"Oh, what lovely flowers!" she exclaimed, and she picked a few to smell.

Then, lying down on the soft grass under a tree, she found there were cherries hanging above her head. She ate a handful to allay her hunger. And thus, with a yawn now and then, she passed the rest of the day.

In the evening when the family came plodding home from their day's work, what did they find? The house not tidied, the water buckets not filled, the fire unlit.

Without a word the old mother threw her hoe into a corner and snatched up the copper bucket. She brought in the water, lit the fire, put the potatoes into a saucepan, and began to knead dough to make a round white loaf. She soon had supper ready. Galinka watched her, sitting on a chair and idly swinging her legs.

When everything was on the table, the mother called her family.

"Come along now, supper's ready!"

Galinka was the first to sit down because she was very hungry. The father took the bread and broke it into three. He handed one piece to his wife and another to his son, and the third he kept for himself.

"And what about the bride?" the mother asked him.

"She is not hungry. If you don't work, you don't get hungry."

Galinka bit her lips and left the table. She went straight to her room and began to weep. She could not sleep, but lay all night long thinking how hungry she was.

The next morning the same thing happened again. This time the vegetable garden had to be planted. Once more Galinka refused to help.

"The sun is too strong," she complained. "I will get sunburned."

So they left her at home. And it simply did not cross Galinka's mind to do anything that day either. She found a dry piece of bread under a plate, left there for the dog. Galinka ate it, and went into the garden to lie on the grass until the evening. But now the lovely flowers were wilting under the hot sun, because she had not watered them.

Later that evening the old parents and their son came home tired out, only to find everything just as they had left it. Once more the mother fetched the water, lit the fire, prepared the dough, and made the bread. When at last they all sat around the table, the father again broke up the bread into three pieces. Galinka's plate remained empty.

"But why don't you give some bread to the bride?" asked the mother.

"Because he that likes to eat bread should first earn it," said the old father calmly, and he began to eat.

All night long Galinka tossed and turned in her bed,

too hungry to sleep. As soon as the cock crowed for the second time next morning, she jumped up and dressed. She looked everywhere for the others, but could not find them. They had gone to the farthest of their fields long before dawn.

Galinka rolled up her sleeves and swept out the house and the yard. She carried water from the well, watered the flowers in the garden, lit the fire, and prepared the supper. She made dough, just as she had seen her mother-in-law do it, and she baked the bread. When all the housework was done, Galinka took the distaff and sat down to spin. It was hard at first, because she had never done it before, but soon Galinka managed to spin an even thread.

In the evening when her young husband and his parents came home exhausted from the day's toil, and saw what the bride had done, their eyes lit up. Galinka laid the table, handed the bread to her father-in-law, and with a heart beating as loud as a drum, waited to see what he would do.

The old man took the bread, in his slow, solemn way, and broke it into four pieces. The biggest piece he gave to Galinka, saying, "Eat, my child, now you have earned your bread. You have been working hard today!"

Galinka took the bread and began to eat it. Never in her life had bread tasted so sweet.

A Man, a Snake, and a Fox

ONE EVENING, as dusk was falling, a man was walking by the riverside. As he walked along he came upon a fisherman gathering up his net. His bag was empty, for he had had no success that day. He had spent the whole day wading in the river, casting his net now here, now there, but not one little fish had he caught.

"Wait a moment," said the passer-by. "Don't go yet. Throw your net into the river once more to try *my* luck. Whatever you catch will be mine, but in return I will give you a golden coin."

The fisherman unfolded his net again and threw it into the deepest part of the river. Then he slowly drew it out and spread it on the sand at the man's feet. Out rolled a jar with a narrow neck, closed by an iron stopper.

The fisherman bent down and picked up the jar.

"It is very heavy. It must be full of gold. Shall I open it?" he said.

"No, don't touch it!" the stranger exclaimed. "The jar is mine. Here is your golden coin. Let me have the jar."

"Oh, my luck's out, that's plain!" sighed the fisherman.

He handed over the jar, took the golden coin, and went away grumbling.

The passer-by looked all around, then took the jar under the bridge where no one would be able to see him, and started to tug at the stopper with trembling hands. His heart was beating very fast. With a great effort he pulled out the iron stopper and peered into the jar. As he did so, a long snake with green eyes slithered out of it and coiled itself over the man's shoulders and around his neck, as if to strangle him.

"Stop! You're strangling me! Stop!" shouted the frightened man.

"I have sworn to strangle the first man that I set eyes on," said the snake. "The man who shut me in the jar was a human being, just like you. Until then I had lived quite peacefully at the bottom of one of his sacks. But one day he found me, pushed me into this jar, and stopped it up tightly, and then threw the jar and me into the river. I have lain on the riverbed for three years. How dreadful that was I will not bore you by telling you, but I nearly died from hunger. There, shut in the darkness of the jar, I swore an oath to strangle the first man I saw. And that happens to be you."

"But I have also saved you! If I had not given the golden coin to the fisherman, you would have remained forever at the bottom of the river. It is not right, you know."

"Not right?" repeated the snake, slightly puzzled. "But if I don't strangle you I shall be breaking my vow!"

"Let us ask the first three people we meet on the road what they think. If they say that you are right to kill the man who saved you, then you can strangle me. But if they say that you are not right, then you must leave my neck alone. Do you agree?"

"Yes, all right," said the snake.

And so the man went on his way, with the snake around his neck—though it had loosened its grip.

First they met a decrepit old horse, so thin you could count his ribs.

"There is the first one," said the man. "You tell him all about it."

The snake stretched its neck toward the horse and began, "I was living quite peacefully at the bottom of a sack when the brother of this man found me and put me in this jar and shut it up with an iron stopper. Then he threw it into the river. I have spent three long years in the jar, rolled into a ball. When I saw, day after day, nothing but black in front of my eyes, I swore an oath that I'd strangle the first man I set eyes on. This man here took the iron stopper out. He is the first man I saw. What do you say—have I the right to strangle him?"

"Go ahead and strangle him," said the horse abruptly.

"Why do you speak like that? What harm have I ever done to you?" cried the man.

"What harm? I'll tell you!" replied the horse. "I was born in a village. My master was a very poor man, and he soon sold me to a rich landowner. My new master coddled me so much that he wouldn't allow a speck of dust to settle on me. Two grooms took care of me. They combed my mane, they gave me fresh water regularly, they fed me on white rice and yellow wheat. My master never went anywhere without me.

"But when I began to grow old he bought another horse, much younger, and ordered the servants to harness me to a cart. I was made to drag wood from the forest, sacks of flour from the mill, and sand and stones for the master's new house. The servants sometimes forgot even to throw a little straw into my manger.

"I toiled for many years, till at last my legs gave way. Once when I was dragging the wagon full of potatoes I stumbled and fell down. When the master saw me he shook his head and said to the servants, 'He is no more use. Better take the knife to him.' The servants unharnessed me and went to sharpen their knives. I just managed to escape into the street and run away. Now do you see how little good I have had from man?"

The man bowed his head and went silently on his way, with the snake around his neck.

After he had walked for some time, a dog came running past.

"Wait! Wait!" cried the snake as the dog raced ahead. "I want to ask you something!"

"Ask quickly, then. I am in a great hurry," said the dog.

The snake told him what had happened and asked if it had the right to strangle the man who had saved it from the river.

"Strangle him!" said the dog. "I've a bone to pick with men."

"What harm have they done to you?" asked the man.

"Great harm. Once I was a pet puppy living in a rich home. The mistress of the house bathed me in the children's bath. I wore a collar with a golden bell. People fondled me and patted me and sat me on their knees at table. They taught me how to stand on my hind legs and beg, and they clapped their hands when I lifted my paws. But as soon as I grew into a big dog they left me in the yard and fed me on scraps from the kitchen.

"Day and night, year after year, I sat guarding the front door. I grew old and went blind in one eye. Then my mistress, who had once held me so lovingly on her knees, said, 'I can't stand a blind dog! Send him away!' So they threw me out. They shut the front door in my face, the door I had guarded all my life. I wandered hopelessly about the town. As soon as I set foot inside a house someone would shout, 'Get hold of that dog and give him a beating he'll remember!' Even the children threw stones at me.

"When I could no longer stand my misery and hunger, I went back to the house where I had lived. The door was open, so I sneaked into the courtyard and toward the kitchen. But my mistress saw me and shouted, 'Can nobody relieve me of that dreadful dog once and for all?' Her sons chased me and belabored me mercilessly with stout sticks. They broke my ribs. I only just managed to escape."

"Now do you see what harm men do?" said the snake, tightening its grip around the man's neck. "They are not kind to us. Why should we treat them better than they treat us?"

"Wait, wait, we must ask a third person. Let us see what he will say," urged the unfortunate man, and he hurried on, his heart sinking.

A fox suddenly trotted out of the bushes, and the man threw up his hands to stop him.

"Aha!" said the fox to himself. "I know what he means by those outspread hands. He is trying to tell me he will give me a chicken for each of his ten fingers if only I'll do something to help him." And aloud he said, "What is the matter?"

"I was caught by a man," began the snake, "and stuffed into a jar with an iron stopper. After shutting me in he threw the jar into the river where I—"

"Wait a minute!" the fox interrupted. "Even a lie has limits. How could a great big snake like you squeeze into a jar? It's not possible!"

"It's true. That's how it was," said the man.

"Maybe, but I won't believe it until I see it with my own eyes. Where is the jar?"

"We left it under the bridge."

"Well, let's go and see if it's possible for such a big snake to squeeze into it."

The three of them went back to the bridge and found the jar.

"Go on, get into it," said the fox.

The snake unwound itself from the man's neck and dropped to the ground with a thud. It crawled tail first into the jar. Soon only the snake's head remained outside.

"There! That proves I'm right!" cried the fox. "There's no room for your head!"

"There is!" shouted the snake, and its head disappeared into the jar.

The fox turned to the man and whispered, "Quick, put in the stopper!"

The man slipped the iron stopper into the neck of the jar and secured it by banging it down with a stone.

"Now throw the jar into this pool," said the fox. "And from now on, don't have anything more to do with snakes."

The man heaved the jar into the pool and thanked the fox gratefully.

"Is that all? What about my ten chickens?" cried the fox.

"What ten chickens? You can have all the chickens in the village if you want them. Just help yourself whenever you're hungry!" said the man.

And that is how the fox got into the habit of visiting the chicken coops each night and taking one or two chickens. He considers he is entitled to them.

Sly Peter at the Fair

WHEN THE FAIR came to town everyone had a holiday. Crowds of people thronged the streets, eating, drinking, and making merry. And Sly Peter was there with all the rest.

As he was wandering about he came to the best inn, facing the big square. He slipped round to the back and peered into the yard, where he saw big caldrons bubbling on the fire. The delicious smell of stew and even the steam that reached Sly Peter's nose sharpened his appetite. He felt an irresistible desire to walk in as a rich man would and taste some of those wonderful dishes which never appeared in his own house, or indeed in his village, or even in his dreams. But how could he do that without a single coin in his empty pocket? And in that particular inn the customers did not pay with copper coins, but with shining silver.

There was really nothing he could do. He might be sly, but he believed himself to be honest, too. And so Peter took a piece of dry bread out of his old bag and held it for a while over the thick steam which was rising from the copper caldrons. He held the bread there until it was moist and fragrant with the appetizing smell of the cooking. Then he ate the bread with great relish and, having finished his meal, moved on.

But he had hardly taken a few steps before the fat innkeeper, who had been watching him silently all the time, cried out, "Hey, you there! You are not going off without paying!"

"Paying? How can you ask me to pay when I haven't eaten anything from your kitchen?" asked the bewildered Peter. "I only moistened my piece of bread over one of those caldrons."

"That is just what you did, I agree," said the innkeeper. "But without fire there is no smoke, and without wood there is no fire. Don't you know that wood has to be paid for?"

As he spoke, the innkeeper's voice grew louder, shriller, and angrier. A small crowd gathered to listen.

"Well, what are you going to do if I tell you that I have no money?" asked Sly Peter.

"In that case I'll give you ten strokes with my stick!"

"All right, bring your stick and give me ten strokes," said Sly Peter. "We'll count them together."

Sly Peter took up a position in the middle of the square. By now the crowd had grown much bigger.

The innkeeper came out waving his stick and made for Sly Peter.

But Peter cried out, "Listen, good people! I haven't touched his food. I only held my own piece of dry bread over the steam of the caldron to moisten it so that I could eat it. This man here insults me and asks me for money.

"The fact is, he has no right to touch me. I haven't

touched his food. But if he insists, he can beat my shadow with his stick and we'll count the ten strokes. Do you agree?"

The onlookers roared with laughter, and chased the innkeeper away.

Silian the Stork

THIS IS A STORY about naughty boys and storks. You
can find both in Bulgaria. You need only walk along a
village street and you will notice them at once.

In the village of Koniar there once lived a peasant
called Bojin, a decent fellow, who had a wife, a daughter,
and a son, Silian. As Silian was the only boy his parents
and his sister spoiled him, attending to his every wish.
Instead of going to school, like all the other children, he
used to run to the river to fish or swim. He disliked working and studying. Pleasure, he thought, was the only thing
for him.

Silian grew into a handsome young man, but his parents did not know what to do with him. The only thing
they could think of was to find him a wife. "If he mar-
ries," they told each other, "he will have to mend his
ways." So they married him to Neda, the nicest girl in the
village; and a year later Silian and Neda had a little boy,
whom the called Velko.

Although Silian was now a married man with a family
of his own, he still hated working. He let his father do

the work on the land, his mother the cooking and mending, and his wife and sister the harvesting. For himself he chose light and pleasant occupations: strolling about in his best clothes, visiting the fair ground in the nearby town, and generally idling away his time. He would eat only white bread and sweet cakes and liked to drink wine with his friends, who were some of the worst liars in those parts.

Bojin, the old father, often remonstrated with his son Silian.

"You choose bad friends, my son, and bad friends will lead you into bad ways!" he would say. "Listen to your parents, or else we shall have to put a curse on you and turn you from our door. Have you heard about the cuckoo and the cat? Once they were human beings, brother and sister, but they refused to obey their parents. So they were cursed and turned into creatures forever living in solitude. If you don't listen to our counsel now, the day will soon come when you, like they, will regret it."

No matter how much his parents begged him to change his ways, Silian would just stare up at the ceiling while they were talking. He did not even bother to listen to them, and, worse still, he did not look his old parents in the eyes. It was great disrespect, of the kind that no Bulgarian peasant would put up with. It pained Bojin to think that a son of his could turn out so badly.

Silian had meanwhile decided to leave the village for good. Without even bidding anyone good-bye, he left his parents' house and made his way to the town, where he

stopped at the best inn for dinner. There he stayed, en-
joying a good meal every day, until he ran out of money;
and after that, when it was time for the next meal, he
had to go hungry.

As luck would have it, just as Silian was beginning to
think he would have to go home again, a monk came to
the inn. He was looking for someone to accompany him
on a pilgrimage to Jerusalem. Silian thought that would
be just the thing for him, and he and the monk set off
together. They spent the summer begging for alms, and
when autumn came they boarded a sailing ship in the
harbor of Salonika.

The wind carried them into the open sea, and the ship
was making good progress when a storm broke. The ship
was tossed up and down by the huge waves, and finally it
was smashed to smithereens against a reef. All the pas-
sengers were drowned, except (as you may have guessed)
Silian. He was holding onto a plank which carried him
to safety.

Once washed ashore Silian lay on the sand for a while,
more dead than alive. His senses were dazed, and with the
noise of the waves in his ears it seemed to him that he
was still floating on the sea. When at last he rose to his
feet, he tried to walk as far from the sea as his legs
would carry him, but after he had walked for a while he
met with the sea again. So Silian started off in another
direction, his back firmly turned to the sea, and once
again he arrived at the seashore.

At long last it dawned on Silian that he was on an

island. He had never been on an island before, and the first thing he wanted to know was whether there were any other living creatures near. He wandered about looking for some houses, but when night fell all he had found was a cave, covered with brambles, with some water bubbling from a spring nearby.

Silian drank some water and ate some berries, and lay down in the cave to sleep. His mind was troubled. Where had he landed? Why was there not a soul about? Why was there no barking of dogs or singing of birds? What kind of an island was this?

Silian began to cry.

"Oh, Mother, my poor mother!" he wailed. "And you, my little Velko! And my darling wife! My dear sister! What are you doing now? Oh, why did I not work in the fields at home, instead of going on a pilgrimage? Why did I not listen to my father? How shall I ever get back to my village when the sea surrounds me on all sides? No matter where I look, there is nothing but water and yet more water!"

And so Silian fretted away the night. When dawn broke, he saw the sun rising up as if from the very bottom of the sea. Silian climbed to the top of a high hill and looked all around him. And there, far away between a slope and a hillock, he suddenly spied a field, with a man and a woman working in it.

Silian made his way toward them as fast as he could. Yes, they were reaping the field. As he approached them he said to himself, "Now, if these two are Bulgarians we

shall understand one another. But what Bulgarian would
want to live on an island in the middle of the sea? They
must be Turks or Greeks, and if so, how am I to make
myself understood?"

He bowed silently to the man and woman, who had
stopped working. To his surprise the man spoke in Bulgarian.

"Welcome, brother Silian!" he said. "You greeted us
without a word. Has fear robbed you of your speech?"

"I wanted to say good day," replied Silian, "but I was
not certain that you spoke my mother tongue. And yet
you even know my name! How is it that you know who
I am? I have never seen you before!"

"The wind, Silian, brought you to our island," said the
man. "We will tell you how we know who you are, but
first you must sit down and eat a little of our bread and
cheese. Then we will go to our house, and you shall be
our guest and hear our story."

Toward dusk the man and the woman led the way to
their home. They had hardly entered the courtyard when
some children ran up to them and began to shout, "Hur-
rah! Here's Silian from Koniar!"

Silian was astonished. "What is this?" he thought to
himself. "Am I dreaming? How do these children know
me? I have never seen them in all my life!"

He followed his host into the house, and everyone
crowded around to welcome him. At table Silian was
treated as a guest of honor and was offered the best
dishes.

After supper some relatives arrived. When they saw Silian sitting there they exclaimed, "Ah, Silian! What good wind brought you here?"

Silian soon realized that the whole village knew him, and as he knew nobody he could not understand it. He was even more surprised when the oldest man in the village started to question him.

"Well, Silian, how is your good father Bojin? Is he in good health? And your kind mother, how is she? Your little son Velko? Your sister Bosilka? Do you still quarrel with your father because you drink too much, or have you given up drinking?"

"Oh, no, I still drink," said Silian. "It was my love of drinking that made me leave my family. If it weren't for that I wouldn't be where I am now. But tell me, how can you know me and my parents?"

"We used to live in your village, Koniar, before you were born," said the old man. "Now we go there every spring and return to the island in the autumn. We have lived in your house and know even better than you all that has happened there. We know everyone in your house, and indeed, in the whole village."

Silian listened with open mouth and wide eyes.

"But how is that possible?" he cried.

"We change into storks every spring," said the old man. "We fly to your village and nest on the roof tops. From there we see everything that goes on in Koniar. And in the evening, when the folk gather together, we listen while they talk."

"But how can you change into storks?" interrupted Silian. "You are human beings, I can see for myself."

"Yes, we are human," the old man sighed. "But we were cursed when we were children, because we were naughty and never listened to our parents. We went about with bad friends and were a nuisance to the whole village. When people scolded us and told us to make ourselves useful we turned a deaf ear.

"One day a stranger appeared in the village. We began to tease and bully him. He grew angry and gave one of us a cuff on the head. So we threw stones at him till one hit him, and he fell dead. The villagers buried him under a plane tree, and as they lowered him into the grave his voice was heard cursing all those who had stoned him to death. That curse transformed us all into storks.

"When autumn came we flew to this island. Here we found two springs of water, and when we bathed in one of them we changed back into human beings. But there was no way of returning to our village till spring came and we could bathe in the water of the other spring to turn ourselves back into storks. And so, year after year, we changed into storks in the spring so that we can fly over the sea to our home."

"But tell me, tell me, please, how am I to return to Koniar?" cried Silian. "Are there no ships that call here?"

"No, Silian, never. Any ship that approaches strikes the reef, as yours did, and breaks up. But I'll tell you how you can return home. When the time comes for us to fly to your village, you must bathe in the spring, as we do.

You will turn into a stork, and you will be able to fly home with us. But your must be sure to fill a bottle with water from the other spring and tie it around your neck, so that when you reach Koniar you can wash yourself and change into a man again."

Silian was still doubtful, so the old man took him to bathe in the spring. Instantly he turned into a stork. He flapped his wings and flew about a little, and then he jumped into the second spring and became a man again.

Silian could not doubt what he saw with his own eyes, and, thinking that he would soon be in his own village, his heart was filled with joy.

"Let me fly straight to Koniar!" he implored the old man.

"No, Silian my boy, that is impossible," the old man replied. "It is winter there, and you know that no stork could stand the cold. Have patience, and when the time comes we will all take wing together."

So Silian had to spend the whole winter on the island. But he was no longer the Silian who would not listen to good advice and refused to work. No, he toiled all day, drank nothing but water, and thought only of the time when he could fly home.

At last the day came. All the inhabitants of the island bathed and changed into storks, and Silian did the same. But he had a bottle of water hung around his neck when he flew with the others to the village of Koniar.

When Silian saw his native village again and flew toward his father's house, he was happy beyond words. In his excitement he forgot the bottle around his neck and rushed forward. He reached the earth below with his head down, so that the bottle hit a stone and broke into pieces. Now Silian had no water to wash himself with, and he would have to remain a stork. Overcome with despair, he started to cry, but it was quite clear that there was nothing he could do.

So Silian flew off and circled around for a while. Soon he alighted on top of his father's house, next to the nest of an old stork. But the old stork turned to him and said, "This is my nest, Silian. Build yours somewhere else. There are plenty of roofs around."

Silian flew on to the next house and from there looked down into his father's courtyard. There was his mother milking a cow, his young wife Neda busy with the sheep, and his sister Bosilka getting wood for the fire. Everybody was working, just as in the old days; and just as in the old days only he, Silian, was doing nothing. He felt that he wanted to be closer to his family, and he flew down into a corner of the courtyard, where there were some young lambs.

But at this moment little Velko, his son, came running out of the house. Seeing the bird he began to scream, "Mother! Mother! The stork is going to take our young lambs!"

"Chase him away, my little one," answered his mother.

Velko took a stone and aimed so well at the head of Silian the stork that he nearly killed him. The poor stork's head began to go round and round. He tried to fly, but could not. And Velko, holding Silian by his long thin legs, screamed, "Mother, Mother, I've caught the stork! Shall I tie him with a string and play with him?"

"Oh, no, my child!" said his mother. "That would be cruel! The stork never does any harm to anyone, only good. Let him alone!"

Velko set the stork free, and Silian flew up and settled on the roof. The next few days he spent building his nest. And so he passed the time, near his family.

One day his father Bojin took his grandson out to the fields with him to drive the oxen. Silian the stork spread his wings and followed them. He came down close to his little son, and looked at the plowshare opening the earth.

"Grandfather, Grandfather, look! There is our stork!" cried Velko.

"Leave him in peace, my boy, he is not in our way!" said the old man.

They both set to work. After a time Velko shouted, "Look, Grandfather, the stork is still following us!"

"Leave him alone, my boy, and drive the oxen a little faster. Night will soon be upon us."

But Velko kept turning to look at the stork, and the old man lost his patience.

"Why do you waste time playing around, silly boy?" he snapped. "I didn't bring you here to look at the stork!"

And Bojin made a move to jab at the oxen with his long stick and at the same time chase away the stork. But by mistake the old man caught him on the leg, and poor

Silian flew away crying out with pain. He landed on his nest with one leg only, the other folded up beneath him.

In the evening the whole family had supper on the veranda. Silian, sitting on his nest, could hear them talking. Little Velko was telling his mother, "Mother, today the stork came with us to the field and Grandfather hit him with his stick. I think he broke his leg."

"It's all your fault, Velko," said old Bojin. "Why did you watch the stork all the time and not pay attention to the oxen? I am sorry it happened. I hit the poor stork by mistake and never meant to do him any harm."

"I'd rather you had given me a cuff on the head," said Velko.

Silian heard all this, and cried and cried.

A few days later he watched his sister Bosilka sitting on a rug in the garden, making a necklace of small silver coins. After threading it, she left it on the rug while she went into the house. Silian promptly flew down and took the necklace in his beak. Then he carried it to his nest on the roof.

A little later his wife came out to sit under the shade of a tree. She began to sew the white blouse of a widow, embroidering it all over with black thread. And all the while she was sadly murmuring to herself, "I would not have grieved half so much if Silian had died here and I knew where his grave was. But he perished at sea, and nobody knows his grave."

Silian could see the tears rolling down Neda's cheeks.

When she got up and went into the house for a handkerchief, he quickly flew down and took a piece of the black thread in his beak to hide in his nest.

A month passed, and it was time for Silian's sister, Bosilka, to be married. The bridegroom arrived with his parents, led by the bagpipes, and all the guests danced themselves to a standstill. Silian watched them from the roof, itching to join them. "Oh, how I should have enjoyed dancing the horo!" he thought.

Neda was the only one who did not take part in the merrymaking or dancing in the gay horo. She went into the shed and cried her heart out. Silian heard her, and his own heart was heavy with pity for his young wife.

Autumn came, and Silian and the other storks had to fly away to the warmer place south. They gathered together on the bank of the river for a grand feast of frogs before they flew off. Their journey took three days and three nights. Silian waited impatiently on the island for another five months until spring came and the storks could return to Koniar once more.

This time when Silian came down in the courtyard of his father's house he was most careful not to break the bottle around his neck. He went straight into the shed and washed himself with the water that transformed storks into men. When he was Silian again he made for the house. Lisa, the dog, saw him but failed to recognize the stranger and barked at him.

"What is the matter, little Lisa? Don't you know your master?" said Silian.

When his family heard his voice they all came running out to embrace him. What a joy it was! Silian took little Velko in his arms and kissed him again and again. He forgot that only last spring Velko had thrown a stone at his head. Father Bojin opened the largest bottle of rakia to celebrate the return of his son, but Silian declined to drink. "I have learned my lesson," he said.

When the old father had recovered from his surprise, he went outside to kill the fattest calf and invite all the neighbors to a feast. While they all ate and drank Silian told them the story of his adventures. Nobody believed a word of it. A man changing into a stork! What a story indeed! They all laughed and laughed.

Without another word Silian went up onto the roof and came back with the necklace of silver coins and the piece of black thread from Neda's blouse. Then he told them how his own father Bojin had hit him with a stick and hurt his leg, and this time it seems they believed what Silian said.

The Clever Billy Goat

ONE HOT SUMMER'S DAY a vixen chased a long-eared
rabbit right up to a deep well in a garden. As he reached
the well, the rabbit gathered all his strength and flew over
it like a bird. The vixen tried to imitate the rabbit's jump,
but instead of going over the well she unexpectedly found
herself at the bottom of it. To her discomfort, the well
turned out to be rather deep, and she could not get out
no matter how she tried. She was almost up to her neck
in cold water, and she began to shiver.

It was not long before a billy goat appeared from the
forest nearby. He came strolling leisurely along, shaking
his beard and waving his horns with a worthy and clever
air.

"What are you doing down there?" he asked, peering
down the well.

"I'm having a nice bath in the cool water," the vixen
replied playfully. "As a matter of fact I am great friends
with the gardener. He invited me to cool off here for a
while. It's such a hot day!"

"Is the water good for a bath?" asked the billy goat.

"Oh, perfect!" cried the vixen in delight, and she ducked her head right under.

"May I jump into the well and have a bath too?"

"Yes, but be careful not to stir up the water."

The bearded billy tumbled head first into the well.

"Oh! Oh! What a clumsy jump!" screeched the vixen. "You've covered my coat with mud! Is that the way to jump in?"

"I don't know of any other way," said the billy goat. "Do you?"

"Yes, and I'll show you the proper way to jump if you'll help me to get out of the well first. Stand up on your hind legs!"

The goat stood on his hind legs while the vixen climbed onto his back, then onto his horns, and then right out of the well.

"Good-bye, stupid!" said the vixen, and waved her paw gaily.

"I am certainly not stupid!" said the billy goat, offended.

"If you were clever you wouldn't be sitting there at the bottom of the well, would you?" said the vixen, and away she ran.

The goat stayed there for three days, and he would have stayed there forever if the gardener had not come along on the fourth day and pulled him out by tying a rope around his neck.

Sly Peter's Revenge

ALL THROUGH THE SUMMER Sly Peter used to take his cow to the lushest meadows. She was so well fed that her coat grew as shiny as a salmon, and Sly Peter decided to take her to the market and sell her.

But three villagers—the innkeeper, the grocer, and the priest—were envious of Peter's fame as the most cunning fellow in the country, and were determined to outwit him and make him a laughing stock. So they put their heads together. The night before Sly Peter was to sell his cow they sneaked out of the village by different roads.

Sly Peter got up very early the next morning and set off to the market with his plump cow. On the way he met the innkeeper.

"Well met, Peter," said the innkeeper. "Where are you taking your cow?"

"To market. Is the market good today?"

"Full. The buyers are falling over one another. You've got a good fat cow, but I'm afraid no one will want to buy her."

"Why not?" asked Sly Peter.

"Because she has a long tail and they are looking for cows without tails in the market."

Sly Peter thoughtfully scratched the nape of his neck.

"That's strange," he said to himself. "I can't understand why they want cows without tails, but if that is what they are looking for, I'll have her tail off. That's easy enough!"

And stopping at a small inn on the road, Sly Peter asked the innkeeper for a pair of shears and cut the cow's tail off. Then he went on his way.

Whom should he meet next but the grocer.

"What do you think?" asked Sly Peter. "Am I likely to find a buyer with a heavy purse for this cow?"

"I think you will. Your cow is without a tail. That's just the kind of cow they are buying in the market. Only her horns will bring the price down."

"Why?" asked Sly Peter.

"Because when the buyers see a beast with horns, they move away."

For the second time that morning Sly Peter scratched the nape of his neck. Without delay he hurried to the next inn, asked for a saw, sawed off the cow's horns, and went on his way.

Shortly before he reached the market Sly Peter met the third schemer, the priest.

"Hurry up, Sly Peter, everybody is going home," said the priest. "But you are a lucky man. In the market today they are bidding everywhere for cows without tails and horns. Still, it would be better if you cut off her ears too."

"What is wrong with her ears?"

"Can't you see? They look just like a donkey's ears."

When the priest had gone, Sly Peter looked at his cow again. "It's true they look a bit like a donkey's ears," he said to himself, and he took out his knife and cut off the poor beast's ears.

When he arrived in the market place, everyone came to stare at the cow. Soon Sly Peter was surrounded by a crowd. They started to laugh at him.

"Look at clever Peter, what a cow he's brought to market! Nobody but a madman would give money for such a beast. Who taught you, Peter, to cut off your cow's tail and her horns and ears? Whoever it was, you must go and kiss his hand when you get home!" they mocked.

Sly Peter wished he could sink into the earth for shame. He pulled the cow out of the laughing crowd and led it to the slaughterhouse, where he sold it to the butcher for next to nothing. And that was the end of his fat cow.

So Sly Peter returned home. The three plotters had already told the whole village about the shorn cow, but Sly Peter said nothing. When his envious friends asked him if he was pleased with his market deal, he smiled broadly and slapped his pocket.

"I'm very pleased indeed. My purse is filled with money. You did me a good turn when you taught me how to prepare my cow so that I could get a double price for it. Now I know you are my real friends. Will you come to supper with me tomorrow evening? I'll get my wife to kill a turkey cock."

"Yes, indeed we'll come," chorused the three friends. "We'll be at your house at dusk tomorrow."

The next day Sly Peter caught two little wild rabbits and put them in a hamper. When darkness fell, he said to his wife, "Wife, I am going to hide in the garden. You receive the guests and tell them I am still in the field. When the turkey is roasted, take one rabbit from the hamper, tell him loudly to come to me in the field, and then let him loose in the road. Leave the rest to me."

The guests arrived early at Sly Peter's house. They sat down on soft cushions and stared greedily at the oven, where a big turkey was roasting. When the turkey was done, Sly Peter's wife picked up her baking shovel and took it out. The three schemers began to lick their lips.

"Oh dear, the turkey is ready, and Peter is late," said the wife.

"Where is he?" asked the innkeeper.

"He went off to the field today. He promised to come back early, but there is no sign of him yet. I think I had better send off the rabbit to call him home."

She lifted one of the rabbits out of the hamper and carried it to the door. In a loud voice, so that the others could hear, she said, "Listen, rabbit, run quickly to the field and tell Peter that the guests have arrived, the turkey is ready, and he must come home at once!"

And she put down the rabbit and let it loose. The

little wild rabbit crossed the yard with a few jumps, went through the front door and into the street, and flew like an arrow toward the fields.

After a while Sly Peter arrived to greet his guests.

"Forgive me," he said, "I'm a bit late. I had a great deal of work to do in the field and forgot the time. I would have been later still if it hadn't been for the rabbit. It came to me out of breath and began to pull at my trouser leg. 'Uncle Peter,' it said, 'you must come home at once. The guests have arrived and the turkey is ready.'"

The guests looked at one another.

"It's the first time we've seen a rabbit as a servant."

"A most useful servant. Yesterday I sent him to town. It took him only two hours, and he came back with a fine new watch I had told him to buy me. Now, let's sit down and start eating before the turkey gets cold."

The guests began to eat. When they had finished, the priest turned to Sly Peter.

"Listen, Peter, why not sell the rabbit?" he said. "I could do with something as useful as that around my house." And the grocer and the innkeeper agreed that they would like to buy it too.

"But there are three of you," said Sly Peter. "How will you share it?"

"That's quite easy," said the priest. "One day it will help me, the next day my friend the grocer, and the day after that the innkeeper. Please, sell us the rabbit!"

"I don't mind selling it," replied Sly Peter, "but it's pretty dear."

"How much do you want?"

"It will cost you as much as a well-fed cow. D'you still want it?"

"Yes, by all means!" cried all three of them. Each took out his purse and counted Sly Peter a whole heap of money.

Sly Peter put the money away. Then he took the other wild rabbit out of the hamper and handed it to his guests, telling them to look after it well, for they would not find another like it in the whole wide world.

The priest took the little rabbit and put it inside his cassock.

"It's mine for tomorrow!" he declared.

Sly Peter saw his guests to the door, and came back grinning. "It serves them right!" he told his wife.

The next day the priest got up early and gave the rabbit some lettuce for breakfast. Then he said, "Listen, my rabbit, go to my friends, those I had supper with at Sly Peter's place, and tell them to come and see us to-night. My wife will make a cheesecake for us all. And hurry, little chap, we have a lot to do today!"

And he led the rabbit out into the street.

The rabbit was soon lost in a cloud of dust. The priest sat on a stool by the front door and waited for the rabbit to return. Noon came, and afternoon too, and then it became dark, but there was still no sign of the rabbit.

Finally the priest got up and went to find his two friends. He asked them why they did not return the rabbit.

"We haven't seen any rabbit," replied the innkeeper and the grocer.

"Where could it have gone to?" said the priest.

"Well, the boy next door told me that last night he saw a rabbit run toward the fields and today he saw another one making for the forest," said the innkeeper.

At last it dawned on all three of them what had happened, and they began to shout, "Sly Peter has cheated us again! What shall we do now?"

"We'll take him to the judge, and get the judge to pass a sentence!"

The very next day the judge, who also had a grudge against Sly Peter, gave his verdict. Sly Peter was to be put in a sack, taken to the cliff, and thrown into the sea. Let him go feed the fish!

"There is nothing you can do about it, Sly Peter, it's fate!" said the three men, opening the sack. "In you go!"

Sly Peter got into the sack and screamed, "But I don't want to! I don't want to!"

"What don't you want to do?"

"I don't want to be thrown into the sea!"

"Well, you're going to be. It's the judge's decision."

And the grocer lifted the sack over his shoulder, calling to his friends, "I'll carry it for a while. When I get tired, one of you can take it. Hup! What a weight!"

And he set off for the sea. The priest and the inn-keeper walked behind, and when the grocer began to groan, they took the sack in turn. They walked and walked until at last, near the sea, they came to a great oak tree. A shepherd was lying under it. It was noon, and his flock were resting in the shade.

"Hi, my friend!" called the grocer. "Is there any water about? We are dying of thirst."

"Yes, at the bottom of the hill," said the shepherd. "You'll find a spring of ice-cold water there."

The carriers left their heavy load on the grass and hurried down the hill. Sly Peter was still repeating from time to time, "I don't want to! I don't want to!"

When the shepherd heard that, he went over to the sack and asked, puzzled, "What don't you want to do?"

"I don't want to become a king," said Sly Peter.

"Why ever not?" said the shepherd.

"Because I am not used to carrying a crown on my head, or eating roast lamb, or sleeping in a feather bed. I don't want to be a king, and that's a fact!"

"But what are you doing in that sack?"

"Those three fellows came to our village and invited me to be king. When I told them I didn't want to be, they caught me and put me in the sack. They want to force me to become king."

"It doesn't sound a bad life to me," said the shepherd.

"Would you like to be king?" asked Sly Peter.

"Well, they haven't asked me," replied the shepherd modestly.

"Tell you what," suggested Sly Peter. "If you'd like to get into the sack, you can be king and I'll be a shepherd instead."

The stupid shepherd eagerly untied the sack and took Sly Peter's place, while Sly Peter went to lie on the grass in the shade of the oak tree.

The three friends soon came back, and the priest took up the sack.

"I want to! I want to!" the shepherd called out from inside the sack.

"What do you want?" asked the priest.

"I want to be king!"

"Poor Sly Peter, he's gone crazy with fear!" said the priest.

He quickly made for the cliff and threw the sack into the sea.

"Good riddance!" said the three friends, and returned to their village.

Toward dusk Sly Peter led the shepherd's flock to his own house. When the three old plotters saw him, they nearly swallowed their tongues.

At last they managed to ask, "Sly Peter, didn't we throw you into the sea today? What are you doing here with all these sheep?"

"I am taking them home," replied Sly Peter. "The sheep are mine!"

"Where did you find them?"

"At the bottom of the sea. There are millions of sheep grazing on seaweed under the water. I took only about a hundred, but when I've sold them I shall go and fetch another hundred."

The grocer jumped up.

"Come on!" he said to his friends.

"Where are you going?" asked the priest.

"Into the sea to get some sheep!"

And they all ran toward the sea. The first to go in was the priest. The other two followed quickly after, and nobody ever saw them again.

The Ungrateful Bear

ONE DAY a peasant went to the forest to collect some wood. As he was walking among the trees he came upon a pit, twice as deep as a man's height, and in the pit was a she-bear. She was growling and stamping to and fro as she waited for the hunter who had dug the trap to come and seize her.

"What are you doing there, old girl?" asked the peasant.

"I fell in head first and now I can't get out. Please, woodcutter, help me out! If you will I'll give you anything you like."

"How can I help you?" said the peasant.

"Put a ladder down the pit," suggested the bear.

"I haven't a ladder, but I could hand you the pole from the cart," the peasant replied. And he lowered the pole into the deep pit.

The old bear climbed carefully up the pole and out of the pit. Then she gave a deep sigh. She had saved her skin.

"Tell me now," she said, turning to the peasant. "What would you like to have for saving my life?"

"I don't want anything," said the peasant.

"No, that is not right," said the bear. "You must have something. Wait! In the hollow of the tree where I live, I keep three earthenware jars of honey. Come with me and take one."

"After all, why shouldn't I take just one?" thought the peasant. He followed the bear to her tree and collected the honey.

As he turned to go home, carrying the jar in his arms, the bear suddenly shouted to him, "That honey is only for you! You must eat it all yourself. You are not to give any of it to anyone else. If you give so much as a mouthful to your wife or children I'll eat you up!"

There was nothing the peasant could do about it, so he cut some wood, piled it on his cart, and went home. When he arrived at his hut his children came running out to meet him. They jumped up and down with excitement when they caught sight of the jar of honey.

"Father, Father, what is in the jar?" they cried.

"Nothing, my children," he replied. "It's empty."

And the peasant unyoked the oxen, took the jar of honey into the cellar, tasted a little of it, and put it away in a dark corner. But as soon as he came up again, the children began to worry him afresh.

"Father, give us a little bit of whatever is in that jar you hid in the cellar!"

The poor peasant said to himself, "It's not right for me to eat all that honey by myself, while the children have none. I am going to let them have some, come what may!"

He brought up the honey from the cellar and said, "I'll give you some of what's in this jar, but first you must go and see that there is nobody about."

The children ran out to look.

"There is nobody about, Father. Only Mother's black dress drying under the roof."

That, had they but known it, was the old bear. She had followed the peasant home and had seen and heard everything.

The children finished the honey and licked their lips. Then they licked the jar clean.

When it was quite empty their father took the jar back to the cellar to hide it again, but the bear was there before him, growling angrily.

"Ho, ho, woodcutter, you didn't keep your word! Now you must go to the river and wash yourself!"

"Whatever for?" said the peasant.

"Because I am going to eat you!"

"Lord! What shall I do now?" thought the peasant, cold with fear. There was nothing he could do. So he made for the river, tears streaming down his face, while the bear prowled along behind.

As he was walking along a fox suddenly appeared in his path.

"Why, what is the matter?" he asked, seeing the peasant's distress.

The peasant told him the whole story from beginning to end. The fox listened carefully and shook his head.

"In the whole story there is just one thing I can't believe," he said.

"What is that?" asked the peasant.

"I can't believe that a bear can climb up a pole."

"I can!" shouted the bear. "I can climb trees and poles, and anything!"

"I am not going to believe that until I see it with my own eyes, not me," said the fox.

"Come along then!" yelled the bear. "I'll show you whether I can or not!"

The fox and the peasant followed the bear into the forest. As soon as they reached the pit the bear shouted, "One, two, three—here I go!"

And—thump!—she jumped into the pit.

"Run along and fetch the pole!" the bear shouted to the peasant.

"Better leave the pole where it is and get the ax instead for this ungrateful bear," said the fox. "You listen to my advice. The next time you see a bear in a pit, don't you hand it a pole!"

Grandmother Marta

ONCE UPON A TIME there was a rich woman who had two girls living in her house. The elder girl was her daughter, the younger her servant.

The woman spoiled her daughter disgracefully. She gave her the whitest of white bread to eat and dressed her in beautiful clothes. She bought her necklaces of colored beads and silver bracelets and gilded slippers from the market. But the little maid, poor girl, had no slippers at all, and her feet were often pricked by thorns. All she had to eat was black rye bread, and instead of a necklace of colored beads she wore just a row of tiny snail shells. She used to collect them herself among the bushes and thread them on a piece of string.

Every day the elder girl slept until noon, and when she woke she was always cross and spiteful. The maidservant had so much work to do that she got up before sunrise. First she had to sweep the house. Then she had to carry the pails through the village to the deep well under the poplar trees, and fill them with clear water.

One night, after the little maid had gone to bed, her mistress came and shook her roughly.

"Get up, girl!" she cried. "I must have some water—I am dying of thirst. Run to the well and get me some! Quickly, now, or you'll be sorry for it."

The girl jumped out of bed, snatched up a jug, and ran as fast as she could toward the well. The streets were deserted, but under the poplar trees, to the girl's surprise, was a group of figures. As she drew closer she saw that there were eleven men and a woman sitting in a circle. They were talking quietly among themselves, and their voices were as gentle as the rustling of leaves.

The girl filled her earthenware jug with water from the well and turned to go home. But at that moment the woman got up and came toward her. She was an old woman, wrinkled and bent.

"Who are you, my child?" she asked.

"I am a servant girl, Grandmother," said the little maid.

"Why do you come so late to fetch water?"

"My mistress sent me here."

"Do you eat wild rose hips?"

"I could eat almost anything!"

"Then take these, my child!" The old woman took a handful of dried rose hips from her bag and handed them to the little maid. The girl smiled shyly and thanked the old woman. Then she ventured to ask, "But who are you, Grandmother?"

"We are the twelve months, my child. I am the month of March, and my name is Grandmother Marta. Every night we come to wash ourselves in the clear water of the well, and then we sit on the soft grass under the poplar trees talking together till the first cock crows and we have to go back to the forest. If anyone passes by while we are here we give him our blessing. We will bless you, too, but first we should like to ask you something."

"Ask me anything you like," the girl said readily.

"Then tell us this. Which is the best month of the year, and which is the worst?"

The young girl pondered for a while. Then she said, "But you are all good! During your month, Grandmother Marta, the lovely snowdrops grow. In the spring months the birds sing and the wheat ripens. In the summer we harvest the golden grain, and in the autumn all the pears, apples, and grapes are ripe for eating."

Grandmother Marta raised her hand and blessed the girl, who had spoken from the goodness of her heart.

"God bless you, dear child!" she said. "When you speak, may golden coins fall from your mouth, and when you smile may flowers blossom on your lips!"

The girl kissed Grandmother Marta's hand gratefully and then ran home. She had hardly crossed the threshold before her mistress shouted furiously, "Why have you been so long, you wicked girl?"

"I was talking to the months," said the little maid. And as she opened her mouth a golden coin fell onto the floor.

Her mistress bent down and picked up the coin. She stared at it in amazement.

"Where did you get this? What have you been doing?"

she cried. And while the girl was telling her about the marvelous blessing of Grandmother Marta, golden coins tumbled one after another out of her mouth and onto the floor. Soon the rich woman had collected a whole plateful.

Now the rich woman ought to have been content with the golden coins that kept showering onto the floor. But she was jealous of the little maid, and she determined that her own daughter, too, must be blessed by Grandmother Marta. So the next night she woke her daughter and told her to go to the well. She washed the girl's face and combed her hair, made her put on her very best dress, her finest necklace, and her gilded slippers, and sent her off through the dark and silent village.

When the girl arrived under the poplar trees the twelve months were already there. They were chatting quietly together, and it was just as though bees were humming.

The girl filled her jug with water. Then she shouted angrily, "Why do you put your heads together like a bunch of old gossips? Speak up! I want to hear what you are talking about!"

Grandmother Marta frowned with displeasure.

"We always talk in this quiet way," she said. "But who are you, girl?"

"That is none of your business!"

"Why have you come in the middle of the night to fetch water?"

"My mother sent me."

"Do you eat dried rose hips?"

"Just you give them to me!" said the girl.

Grandmother Marta took some rose hips from her bag and handed them to the girl. She grabbed them without a word and threw them straight into the eyes of the old woman. Then she burst out laughing. A little sparrow, asleep in its nest, was so startled that it fell onto the ground.

Grandmother Marta only bit her lips and said nothing. After a while she broke the silence.

"I will ask you something, my girl, and you must answer me truthfully," she said.

"Ask away," said the girl carelessly.

"Which is the best month of the year, and which the worst?"

"They are all bad," replied the girl without hesitation. "During the winter months of ice and frost we can't show our noses outside. In the foolish month of March it is always raining or snowing or thawing. During the summer months it is so hot that the flies and mosquitoes never stop biting you. And in the autumn the leaves turn yellow and begin to fall, and everything is miserable."

"Is that so?" said Grandmother Marta. "Then listen to my blessing. When you speak, may snakes and lizards crawl out of your mouth, and when you smile may nettles blossom on your lips!"

The girl picked up her jug and marched home in a furious temper. Her mother was waiting for her at the door. She ran forward to embrace her daughter.

"Talk, my darling, talk, my sweet child, and I will collect all the golden coins in my apron," she cried.

"What is there to talk about?" said the girl sulkily. And the moment she opened her mouth snakes and lizards started to drop into her mother's apron.

The rich woman turned green with fury. She snatched up a stick and began to beat the little maidservant mercilessly.

"You horrid girl!" she screamed. "Why did you not tell my daughter what to say to the months so that she could be blessed like you?"

When her mistress had finished beating her, the little maid slipped quickly out of the house. She sat down on a stone and began to cry.

It was still early morning, but before long a handsome young man came by. When he saw the girl sitting there crying, he stopped.

"Have you lost your way?" he asked. And the girl lifted her head and smiled at him, and on her lips blossomed flowers. The young man could not help but fall in love with her, and he took her to be his wife.

But the bad girl continued to drop snakes and lizards from her mouth whenever she spoke, and nettles still bloomed on her lips when she smiled.

As for Grandmother Marta—well, now you know to think twice before you find fault with the weather.

The Escape of the Animals

A PEASANT WORKS HARD, but his animals often work harder still. That is so at least with Bulgarian peasants and animals. And one day it happened that the long-suffering donkey lost his patience, took to his heels, and made off to the forest.

On the way he met the old ram, who stopped the donkey to ask, "Why are you running away, my friend?"

"I am running away from People," said the donkey.

"But why? What is the matter?"

The donkey lifted his big, honest eyes to the sky and gave a very long sigh, as only donkeys can.

"I can't stand it any longer," he said. "I tell you I've had more than enough. When autumn comes they say, 'Donkey, carry these baskets of apples!' In the winter it's 'Donkey, bring in the wood!' And as soon as spring is upon us again, 'Donkey, carry these boxes of eggs!' And do you know what they give me to eat? They throw me a handful of dry vine leaves, if you please! No, People don't really care whether I live or die. So I've decided to escape. I'm going to run away to some place where donkeys live without working, and I shall stay there for the rest of my life."

The old ram shook his curling horns and cried, "Oh, brother, brother, I am taking myself off for the very same reason! Whenever a marriage is being arranged they say, 'Let's catch the ram and prepare a grand feast for the wedding guests!' And when there is a funeral, it's the same thing: 'We'll have to kill the old ram in memory of the dead,' they solemnly declare. Even if it's only some friend arriving they look in my direction and say, 'It wouldn't be a bad idea to kill the ram and give our friend a really good meal.' I have put up with my fears for so long that today I felt I couldn't bear it any longer, and I ran away. Do you think, my friend, we could run away together?"

"Why not? We can travel together and defend each other if anybody attacks us," replied the donkey happily.

They walked for a while until, in a little valley, they met the fox.

"Where are you going?" asked the archenemy of all chickens.

"We are running away."

"You don't mean to say you are running away from your master?"

The donkey and the ram told him all about their troubles.

"Oh!" cried the fox. "That is a funny thing! You would hardly believe it, but I'm running away for the same reason. Whenever I hear People beating a wedding drum, my heart starts to beat too. I know only too well that the bridegroom will do anything to slip the skin off my back for a lovely fur coat for his bride. Would you like me to come with you?"

"Yes, please come with us!" replied the two runaways, and they set off again with the fox following them.

Soon they came to a wood, where they met a young cockerel. He was strutting about under the trees, peering anxiously around.

"Thank goodness!" cried the cockerel. "At last some living souls in this deserted wood! Where are you going, my friends?"

The donkey, the ram, and the fox told him where they came from and why they were running away.

"And you, young cockerel, what are you doing all alone?" they asked.

"Just the same as you, my dear fellows, I am running away! I have a very good reason, too, for leaving home. When the first baby is born in the family, the father says, 'I'll catch the cockerel and we'll have him for the christening feast!' And whenever there is a birthday, it's 'Let's have roast cockerel for this special day!' Even if it's only mother-in-law coming for a visit, it's the pot for me! They don't care whether I'm grown up or whether I can crow, all they think about is how to put me on the table. Oh, please, please, do take me with you!" begged the young cockerel.

So the three became four and went on their way.

They walked and walked till they came to a crossroads,

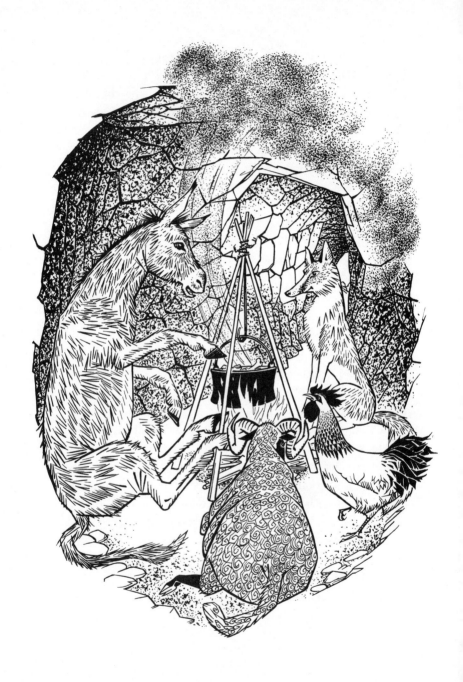

and what do you think they saw there? The skin of a wolf, of all things, lying in the middle of the road!

They sniffed at it, jumped over it, and came back to sniff it again.

"Why not take it with us?" suggested the ram. "It might bring us luck!"

"But who is going to carry it?" asked the cockerel.

"I'll carry it!" said the donkey. "Just fling it on my back."

They threw the skin over his back and continued on their way. Toward dusk, after they had wandered for a long time through the wood, they came to a cave. They looked inside. There was no one there, and they went in. Right in the middle of the cave they found a fire, and over the fire a big saucepan full of stew. Our travelers sat down around the fire to warm themselves.

"It is very cozy here," they all agreed. "And when the owners come back, if they are good people they may give us something to eat. Maybe we could spend the night here, and go on our way again tomorrow." They were all in a mellow mood, and felt very comfortable.

Suddenly the donkey remembered that the wolf's skin was still outside, and very likely getting damp. So they filled it with straw and hung it up under the trees at the entrance of the cave to dry.

And who were our travelers' hosts? Well, there lived in this particular cave two families, one of wolves and one of bears. After stoking the fire and putting the stew to cook, they had gone out, as usual, to hunt for a while until their supper was ready. And it was not long before they arrived home.

The sight of the bears and wolves coming into the cave so frightened the uninvited guests that they almost swallowed their tongues in terror.

"Welcome, welcome, dear guests!" growled the bears and the wolves in some excitement.

"How do you do?" replied their guests politely, in quavering voices.

The oldest bear was bustling about. She brought out some spoons and invited her guests to sit down.

"Come along!" she said. "Take your seats around the table. Don't be shy!"

The guests sat down and helped themselves to the stew. When the pot was empty, the old she-bear said, "As you come from the villages, where we have never been, you must know some very good songs. We have heard that People have jolly weddings and dances. So let's hear you sing!"

"We are quite willing to sing," said the donkey, "but according to custom it is the host who must sing first."

"I'll sing if you like!" cried the old she-bear, and she burst into song in a deep, rusty voice. You could tell she had not sung much before. It was not exactly a song—it was more like a growl. And what she sang was what was uppermost in her mind.

> If a meal walks in
> When the hunter's out

It will lose its skin
Without any doubt.

When the runaways heard the words of the song their teeth began to chatter with fear. What else could this be but a grim warning? The poor donkey had to sing next, and he was certainly not in the mood for singing, but what could he do? He just managed to bray this song in a trembling voice.

Do go out and see
What hangs from the tree
In front of your house.
It isn't a mouse.

When the wolves and bears heard this strange song, they told a little bear to go out and see what was hanging in front of the cave. The old she-bear added, "If you see something good, come back at once and tell us. But if you see something bad, run fast and don't come back!"

The little bear crept timidly out—and what did he see? Just in front of the cave a strangled wolf was hanging from a tree. The poor little bear gave one terrified yelp and ran off as fast as his legs would carry him, all the way to the top of the mountain.

After a time the old wolf decided to send out one of his little wolves. The two families waited for a while, and then the old bear gave a push to another of her little bears.

"*You* go out and see what's hanging in front of the cave!"

And so, one after another, all the little bears and wolves went out, and not a single one of them came back. At last, when it was quite dark, the old wolf and the old she-bear thought it was time they got up to see what had happened to their children. But the moment they moved, their frightened guests thought their last minute had come, and they jumped to their feet in a terrible panic. The ram got his horns stuck in the doorway. The old bear roared. The donkey began to bray, as all donkeys do. The cockerel flew up to the shelf and crowed his head off. The fox howled and dived into a big jug.

At last the ram managed to free himself, and the bear and the wolf scrambled hastily through the doorway. As soon as they set eyes on the hanging wolf they rushed into the wood, frightened almost out of their wits. They never stopped running until they had crashed through nine forests and come to the edge of the tenth. Here they halted, panting.

When the bear had got her breath back, she exclaimed, "My goodness! Wasn't that terrible? I haven't yet come to my senses! Wolf, did you see the little one with the red comb jump onto the shelf looking for a knife?"

"And did you notice how the other one, with the long tail, leaped into the jug looking for a rope to hang us with?" said the wolf, still shaking with fright.

"Thank goodness we are rid of our terrible guests at last!" said the old bear. And she and the wolf made their way into the mountain to search in all the hollow trees for their lost children.

The donkey, the ram, and the cockerel all decided that the woods were much more dangerous than the villages, and so they went back to live among People.

But the poor fox stayed in the jug.

Silver Leaves and Golden Blossom

ONCE UPON A TIME there was a miller who had three daughters. The two elder could hardly be called beautiful, but the youngest was as lovely as the evening star.

One evening the three sisters took their spinning wheels to the front of the mill and sat down to spin by moonlight. And as they spun they talked.

Said the eldest sister, "If the Voyvoda's son chose me for his wife I'd spin him enough wool from one distaff to clothe the whole of his army."

Said the second sister, "If he took me for his wife I'd knead him enough white bread to feed the whole of his army."

And the third sister, the little one, said, "If the Voyvoda's son married me I'd give him two sons with golden hair and silver teeth."

Now every evening the Voyvoda's son used to ride past the mill as he took his white horse to the river. This time he happened to pass by while the three girls were sitting outside spinning and talking, and he could not help hearing what they said.

As he rode past again on his way back from the river he went into the mill to see the old miller.

"Miller," he said, "I want to marry one of your daughters. Will you give her to me?"

"Which one do you want?" asked the miller, overjoyed.

"The little one."

"Then take her, son, but tell me first what your craft is."

"I am the Voyvoda's son. My father is old, and if I marry he will give me command of the whole army. Then I shall be the Voyvoda."

"Well," said the miller, "if what you say is true then it's all right with me."

The next day was a Friday, and the Voyvoda's son decided to celebrate his wedding at once. He drove up to the mill in a golden carriage and took the miller's youngest daughter away to his father's palace. Here they lived happily together. When the old father retired from the Czar's service he was succeeded by his son, who made a good Voyvoda.

One day the miller's two elder daughters arrived at the palace.

"Dear sister," they begged, "take us into the palace so that we too may have a better life. We are so tired of being always covered with flour. We hate Father's mill. It's not a bit like your palace!"

"Of course you must come to live here," replied the Voyvoda's young wife, and she settled them in the palace.

The second sister soon found a good husband and went to live in her own home. But the eldest sister remained at the palace, and she carried envy in her heart like a coiled serpent. Day and night she mooned through the rooms of the palace, wondering how she could drive her little sister away and marry the Voyvoda herself.

One day the Voyvoda left the palace to go hunting, and while he was away his young wife gave birth to two children—beautiful little boys with golden hair and silver teeth. Looking at her lovely babies the little mother was so happy that her eyes filled with tears.

The eldest sister stood near the little mother's bed, bursting with envy. At last she said, "Sister, why don't you have a little sleep? You look tired."

"But what about the babies?" asked the mother.

"I will take care of them. I will put them in the cradle and rock them to sleep."

The young mother thanked her sister gratefully and closed her eyes. As soon as she was asleep her envious sister snatched up the newborn babies and ran outside to the darkest corner of the garden, and there she killed them and buried them. Her only witness was the palace cat, who was out hunting. In the empty cradle she put two puppies, and sat down by their side, singing to them and rocking them. The young mother slept on.

At midnight the Voyvoda returned. The eldest sister was the first to greet him.

"You are a father now, Voyvoda."

"Let me see! Is it a boy or a girl?" cried the Voyvoda.

He ran to the cradle—and saw the two puppies. He was beside himself with anger. He turned yellow with rage and shouted, "Out! Throw those puppies away! And throw out the mother too! Build her a straw hut somewhere by the river and let her live there. From now on she can look after my ducks."

"And what are you going to do without a wife?" asked the envious sister slyly.

"That is quite simple!" snapped the Voyvoda. "I'll marry you!"

And the very same night his order was carried out.

The next morning the Voyvoda went for a walk in his garden, and what do you think he saw? At the spot where the envious sister had buried the two children there now grew two beautiful trees, with silver leaves and golden blossoms. The Voyvoda was amazed. He called to his new wife, "Come and look! A miracle has happened!"

As he passed under the trees, the branches bent down and caressed his head. But as his new wife passed under them the branches bent down and lashed her face.

The Voyvoda sent for some joiners and ordered them to fix two beds between the branches of the two trees.

"Tonight my wife and I will sleep up there, among the silver leaves and golden blossoms," he said.

The joiners did as he had told them, and that night the Voyvoda and his wife lay down to sleep in the trees, with the silver leaves rustling above their heads.

The Voyvoda quickly fell asleep, his face gently

caressed by the blossoms. But his wife lay wide awake, and felt as if she were lying on thistles. She could not even close her eyes, for the branches beat against her face.

Toward midnight the two trees spoke to each other in human voices.

"Brother," said one, "is the Voyvoda heavy?"

"He doesn't feel heavy, because he is my father," replied the other. "He is as light as a feather. Is his wife heavy?"

"As heavy as a buffalo. My branches are cracking."

When the Voyvoda's wife heard this she climbed down from the tree and spent the rest of the night on the wet grass.

The next day, while the Voyvoda was out hunting, his wife took an ax and cut down the trees and burned them. Only a small heap of ash remained. The duck girl, whose children the trees had been, scooped up a handful of ashes and scattered them among the flower beds. By evening a lovely basil plant with golden tips had shot up.

The envious sister guessed that the basil must have grown up out of the ashes, and so she let a ewe into the garden. The ewe nibbled off all the basil; that night she gave birth to two lambs with silver wool and golden horns.

When the Voyvoda's wife saw the lambs, she picked them up, put them into a basket, sealed it with resin, and threw it into the river. The basket was carried downstream until it caught in the willow that grew in front of the straw hut where the duck girl lived.

It was nighttime, and the lambs were hungry. They

began to bleat sadly. The duck girl, hearing them, got up and lit a candle. She hurried out to the willow, and there she saw the sealed basket. She was surprised to find inside it two silver lambs with golden horns—but she knew at once that these were her own babies, so she took them into the hut and gave them some milk. And as soon as they had drunk the milk the two lambs turned into two boys, with golden hair and silver teeth.

The boys with the golden hair and silver teeth stayed in the straw hut with their mother until they were three years old. When they played outside, everyone who passed by the hut stopped to marvel at their beauty.

Once the Voyvoda's wife walked by. When the children saw her they threw stones at her. But another time the Voyvoda himself rode by, and the boys ran out with two brooms and swept the path before his horse.

The Voyvoda was greatly astonished when he saw the two little boys with silver teeth and golden hair—just like those that once the miller's daughter had promised to give him. Something stirred in his heart. He went to look for the duck girl. She was by the river minding the ducks, with a long stick in her hand.

"Where did you get those children?" asked the Voyvoda.

"I found them in a basket floating in the river," the duck girl replied.

Puzzled, the Voyvoda returned to his palace, and there he found his wife running after a cat to beat it for helping itself to some milk.

"Don't you hit me, or I'll tell the Voyvoda how you killed the babies and put puppies in their place," mewed the cat.

When the Voyvoda heard this he snatched the stick from his wife's hand and threw it out of the window. He picked up the cat and asked it what it meant. The cat had seen everything. It told the Voyvoda all that had happened, from beginning to end—how his wife had killed the children and cut down the trees, how she had got the ewe to eat the basil plant, and how she had put the lambs in a basket.

"And how did the lambs turn into babies?" asked the Voyvoda.

"I saw that too," said the cat, "as I went to hunt for mice in the hut by the river. I was there when the duck girl opened the basket. As soon as she gave mother's milk to the lambs, they both turned into babies again."

When the cat had finished its story, the Voyvoda jumped onto his horse and rode to the hut by the river to fetch his first wife and his two sons. But the eldest sister he ordered to be put in a barrel sealed with resin and thrown into the sea.

The Bag of Lies

NASREDIN HODJA WAS a Turk who was famous for being a great liar. He told lies wherever he went, and when he had lied to everyone in Anatolia he decided to go and deceive the simple people of Bulgaria.

One day he arrived at the village where Sly Peter lived. In the street, leaning against the fence around the priest's house, stood Sly Peter himself.

Nasredin Hodja was the first to speak.

"Are you Sly Peter?" he asked.

"I am indeed," answered Sly Peter.

"I have heard people say that you are the greatest liar in the world."

"That is just idle gossip," said Sly Peter modestly. "I have heard the same about you."

"What are you doing here?" asked the Hodja.

"I am holding up this fence. If I didn't it would fall down."

"Shall we try to outlie each other?" said the Hodja.

"Why not?" said Sly Peter. "I can't start just now, because I have left my lies at home. I always carry them about in a bag, and when I don't need them I keep them hanging on the wall. If you'd like to hold up the fence for a while, I'll run home to fetch the bag and then we'll start."

"Go then," said Nasredin Hodja, "and be quick!"

Sly Peter made off down the hill and slipped into a coffee shop to have coffee. Meanwhile the Hodja remained leaning against the priest's fence, holding it up, waiting for Sly Peter to come back. He waited and waited, till it grew dusk and then dark. At last he went angrily away.

The next day Nasredin Hodja met Sly Peter again.

"What do you mean by it, Peter, why didn't you turn up yesterday?" shouted the Hodja. "You promised to bring your bag of lies and then you disappeared altogether."

"Hodja," replied Sly Peter, "what bigger lie do you want than that? I left you to hold up the fence all day long waiting for me."

Nesredin Hodja bit his lip. He was furious.

"You are not angry, are you?" said Sly Peter. "Let's go for a walk in the forest under the shady trees where the bears find their honey, and when you feel better we'll try to outwit each other again."

The Hodja agreed and they set off. They strolled out of the village talking, and at length reached the forest.

"At home," the Hodja was saying, "we have two suns shining. We have winged donkeys and the rabbits lay their eggs in nests at the top of the highest trees."

"You tell wonderful lies, Hodja," said Sly Peter, "but I don't believe you."

"Our water is dry," continued the Hodja. "We don't drink it, we cut it with a knife."

"That is a good try, Hodja, but I still don't believe a word."

They disappeared into the thick of the forest. Noon turned over. They were both hungry.

"We ought to have a bite of something," said Sly Peter.

"What shall we have?" asked Nasredin Hodja.

"I don't know. There is nothing here we can eat," said Sly Peter, looking around.

At that moment a young farmer came along, carrying a young lamb over one shoulder.

"Now, do you think I could get that lamb?" asked Sly Peter.

"I shouldn't think so," said the Hodja. "The farmer is young and strong. I don't believe you could beat him."

"You wait here a little. Just watch and keep quiet!"

Sly Peter slipped into the thicket, ran ahead of the farmer, and dropped one of his sandals in the middle of the path. Then he ran a hundred yards further and dropped his other sandal.

When the young farmer reached the first sandal, he kicked it away and said to himself, "Not a bad sandal, but what use is only one to me?"

Soon he came to the second sandal.

"Well, well, another sandal!" he thought. "I must go

back and fetch the first one." So he lifted the lamb from his shoulder and left it on the path while he went back.

But Sly Peter, who had in the meantime collected the first sandal, jumped out of the thicket, snatched up the lamb, collected the other sandal, and returned to the Hodja.

The Hodja was bursting with envy when he saw what an accomplished trickster Sly Peter was.

Sly Peter and the Hodja made a good fire, killed the lamb, and roasted it. Then they sat down to eat.

"Hodja," said Sly Peter suddenly, "I could drive you away from here with lies before you could eat one mouthful."

"You couldn't possibly!" said the Hodja.

"I could."

"Then let's see you do it."

"I'll show you in a minute. Just wait until we've put some salt on the roast. Look! Down in the dale there is some salted earth. I'll run and fetch a handful, and when we've salted the lamb I'll cheat you out of it."

"Be quick! I am terribly hungry," said the Hodja, devouring the roast lamb with his eyes.

Sly Peter went down into the dell, out of sight of the Hodja. Suddenly he screamed, "Oh! Ah! Help! Don't beat me! It isn't me! Oh! It's the Hodja who stole your lamb. There he is, up there! You go and ask him where the lamb is!"

When Nasredin Hodja heard these cries, he jumped to his feet, thinking, "It's that thick-necked farmer! He'll break every bone in my body. I must be off before he finds me!"

And he ran off as fast as a horse, with sparks flying from under his feet.

So Sly Peter came out of the dell and ate the roast lamb all by himself.

The Precious Stone

GRANDFATHER PAVEL was a simple plowman whose home was in the Old Mountain. He had a hut with a slate roof, a kitten, a duck, and ten sheep. All he lacked was a lamp to give light while he ate his supper.

One day Grandfather Pavel was walking behind his flock over a soft meadow near the forest when he heard what sounded like a sad song on a willow pipe, coming from a thicket. He made his way into the thicket to find out what it was, and saw that the wood was burning and crackling. A little spotted lizard was twitching and screaming near a burning stump.

"Plowman," pleaded the lizard, "be my friend and help me out of the fire."

"I would gladly help you, but I cannot reach you without burning my feet."

"Then hold out your stick. I will cling to it and you can pull me out."

Grandfather Pavel stretched out his shepherd's crook. The lizard twisted itself around it and came safely out of the fire.

"I must reward you," said the little lizard gratefully, when it had recovered. "Follow me!"

"How can you reward me?" asked Grandfather Pavel.

"My father is King Lizard, and he lives in a deep, dark cave. In his crown there are nine precious stones, shining like nine suns. I shall give you one of them."

The little lizard darted into the grass toward the river, and the old man hurried after. At last they came to a cave.

"Now you wait here while I go and get the stone," said the little lizard.

Grandfather sat down on the ground. Dusk was already falling, and by the time the little lizard came back it was quite dark. When at last it appeared, it was carrying the precious stone in its mouth; and from the stone shone a great light, so that at once the whole meadow was lit up. The birds in the trees nearby, thinking that it was daybreak and the sun was shining, spread their wings and started to chirrup.

"Take this stone back to your hut," said the lizard. "When you get there, tap the stone on the ground three times and say what you want to have. Whatever your wish, it will be fulfilled."

Grandfather Pavel took the stone in his hand and looked at it. It was no bigger than a hazelnut. He dropped it in his bag and turned to go home. He found his flock still grazing, and the kitten and the duck waiting for him at the front door.

The old man rounded up the sheep, and only when he

was inside the hut did he take out the stone again. It was suddenly so bright in the hut that the kitten covered her eyes with her paws and the duck tucked her head under her wing.

Grandfather Pavel had his supper. Then he said to himself, "Why should I ask the stone for anything more when I have all I need? I have a hut and sheep and cheese, and now even a light to shine on my table."

And so he went to bed. But sleep would not come to him, and he began to think about the stone.

"Why should I not just test the little stone?" he thought. "Why shouldn't I ask for something? I wonder what I'd like to have. Well, why not a marble palace?"

And while he was saying the words, he tapped the stone on the ground three times. At once the hut vanished, and in its place there was a marble palace. The walls were made of mirrors, the pots and pans of pure gold, and the tables and chairs of ivory. The old man, bewildered, went from room to room gazing at everything in wonderment. At last he sank onto a soft, downy bed, carefully putting the stone inside his shirt.

As luck would have it, at that very moment his neighbor Ivan came to visit him.

"I came to see if you were still alive, and to have a little chat with you," said Ivan. "But I can't believe my eyes! What miracle is this? Who built this palace for you?"

"A little stone built it," said Grandfather Pavel.

"A stone? What stone? Let me see it!"

Grandfather Pavel drew the stone from his shirt and handed it to Ivan. Ivan examined it carefully.

"And how did this little stone manage to build a palace?" he asked.

Grandfather Pavel told him the whole story—though he took care to put the stone back in his shirt first. They sat chatting until they began to yawn.

"You had better spend the night here, Ivan," said Grandfather Pavel. "Lie next to me on this downy bed."

Ivan lay down as if to sleep. As soon as Grandfather Pavel was asleep he put his hand inside the old man's shirt and took out the stone. Tapping it three times on the ground, he said, "I want four giants to lift this palace and take it away right to the other side of the Danube!"

Sure enough, while he was still saying this, four giants appeared before him. They heaved the palace onto their shoulders and carried it away, followed by Ivan, who was still holding the precious stone.

But poor Grandfather Pavel was left behind. When he woke up in the morning and looked around there was no trace of a palace, and no trace of the precious stone either—only the shabby old hut with the slate roof and the kitten and the duck. Tears began to run down Grandfather Pavel's old cheeks. Even the sheep felt sorry for him and bleatedly sadly. The kitten felt miserable and the duck was very angry.

"Let us go and look for Grandfather's stone on the other side of the Danube," suggested the kitten.

"Yes, let's," said the duck.

They walked a long way, right across the green plain until they came to the broad and softly flowing Danube.

"I can swim," said the duck, "but you can't. Jump on my back and I will carry you across."

The kitten perched on the duck's back, and the duck swam across the river. When they had walked a little further on the other side they saw Grandfather Pavel's marble palace.

"Let's wait outside until dark," said the kitten. "Then we can go in without Ivan seeing us."

They hid in the garden till darkness fell, and then climbed through an open window. They found Ivan asleep on the downy bed, with the precious stone hidden under his tongue. They knew it was there because a light was shining in his throat.

"How shall we get it out?" asked the duck.

"I'll tell you how," said the kitten. "I'll dip my tail into the pepper pot and then tickle his nose with it. Ivan will sneeze and the stone will jump out of his mouth."

No sooner said than done. The kitten flicked her peppery tail under Ivan's nose, and when Ivan sneezed the stone flew out. The kitten grabbed it, and she and the duck shot out of the window again and didn't stop running until they reached the shore of the Danube. Then the kitten once more jumped onto the duck's back, and the duck waded into the water.

Halfway across the duck said, "What is this miraculous stone? Let me see it!"

"You can't see it now—you might drop it in the water. You can see it when we are ashore," said the kitten.

"If you don't give it to me now I'll go under water and you will be drowned," quacked the duck.

The kitten was frightened. "Here, take it!" she said.

So the duck held out her webbed foot to take the stone and plonk! it dropped into the water. The two little creatures came ashore and burst into tears.

Now just at that moment a fisherman passed by, and seeing them he stopped and said, "Why are you crying?"

"We are so hungry!" wept the kitten.

The fisherman threw his net into the water and landed a big fish.

"Here you are," he said. "Now you need cry no more."

The kitten and the duck carried off their fish and sat down under a willow, and when they had eaten a little of it, what do you think they found? Inside the fish was the precious stone! The fish had been swimming nearby when the duck dropped the stone, and would you believe it—the stone had fallen straight into its open mouth!

The little creatures were beside themselves with joy. They set off across the green Danube plain once more and did not stop until they reached Grandfather's hut in the Old Mountain. The old man was still sitting on the ground weeping when they rolled the little stone right up to his nose.

Grandfather Pavel's eyes lit up when he saw it, and he snatched it up and knocked three times on the ground, crying, "Send me Ivan, tied up in a sack!"

Even while he was saying the words a large sack appeared, with Ivan kicking inside it. Grandfather Pavel picked up his stick and gave him a good beating. Then he untied the sack and sent Ivan home.

"I won't have another palace. Ivan would be sure to

come and steal it, I know him too well," said Grandfather
Pavel to himself, and he hid the stone at the bottom of
his bag.

So he went on looking after his sheep just as before, and
every night he took out the precious stone and put it on
the shelf to give him light. And when Grandfather Pavel
died at a very old age, the little lizard came to the hut
and took the stone back.

The Lazy One

ONCE UPON A TIME there was a very lazy man. He would lie all day long in the shade while his children went hungry and had to go from house to house begging food. Passers-by would stop and scold him.

"You ought to be ashamed of yourself! Your children, poor waifs, wander about not knowing where their next meal is coming from. Everyone else works hard, and you are the only one who idles away his time. Do some work!"

"Don't want to," the lazy man would say, and he would turn over on the other side.

At last the lazy man could stand it no longer. He actually got up on his feet and went to see the village priest.

"Father," he said, "I want you to do the funeral rites for me. Call the villagers and tell them to bury me alive."

"Whatever for?" asked the priest, astonished.

"Because I am tired of people always finding fault with me. They won't leave me in peace. They scold me every day because I don't work. If I go into the next world, at least I can lie undisturbed."

"Very well," said the priest. He performed the funeral

rites and called two men to carry the lazy man's bier to
the graveyard.

On their way there, they met a hard-working peasant.

"Where are you taking that man?" he asked.

"To the graveyard to bury him."

"But you can't do that! You can't bury someone who is alive! Who told you to do such a crazy thing?"

The two men told the story.

"Get up!" said the hard-working man to the lazy one. "Come home with me and I'll give you a bit of corn so that you can have something to eat before you start to earn your bread."

The lazy one raised himself a little and asked, "Will you give it to me ground?"

"That's a fine thing to ask! I'm not going to grind it for you!"

"In that case," said the lazy man, turning to the bearers, "just go on. Straight to the graveyard. That corn is no good to me. First I should have to take it to the mill to have it ground, then bring it home, mix it, knead it, bake it, eat it—oh no, it's such a long business! I shall be better off in the graveyard."

So to the graveyard they took him. They dug a hole and lowered the lazy man into it. Then they threw some earth over him, but they put a little pipe from his mouth to the ground above so that he could breathe. The priest came to read the last rites over him and then went off with the two gravediggers.

During the night the hard-working peasant woke up thinking about the lazy one. "I'll go and cure that man of laziness once and for all," he said to himself. He jumped out of bed and put on some black clothes. He blackened his face with soot and fixed a pair of horns on his head. Then he went to the graveyard, where he began to dig the lazy man out.

"Get up, you!" he shouted, giving the lazy one a kick. "I am the devil. Today as we were sorting out the souls of the dead I got yours. I am your master now. Whatever I order you to do you must obey—and if you don't I'll put you to boil in a caldron full of hot tar. You've done enough of this lying about!"

The lazy man began to tremble with fear.

"What work do I have to do?" he asked.

"At the other end of the graveyard you'll find a big heap of stones. Bring them all up here to this end. Go on! I want all those stones brought up here before dawn."

The lazy man at once set about carrying the heavy stones from one end of the graveyard to the other, lifting and carrying, panting and puffing, tripping, falling, and getting up again. When he had taken the last stone across the graveyard, the man dressed as the devil appeared again. This time he was holding a stick in his hand.

"Come here and I'll give you your pay!" he said, and seizing the lazy man he tied him up against a tree and gave him a sound thrashing. "That is how the devil pays his servants!" he said at last, throwing down his stick. "Now, back to the grave!" And he untied the lazy one and dragged him back to his hole.

The lazy one lay down. His tormentor threw a couple of shovels of earth over him and went away. Dawn broke. The buried man, slowly recovering, moved a bit. Discovering that there was only a little earth over him he jumped out of the grave and quickly made for the village. When he reached home he grabbed an ax, went into the forest, still panting from his run, and began cutting wood.

A peasant passed by and greeted him jokingly.

"Good day, friend. What news from the next world?"

"Don't you be in a hurry to go there," said the lazy one solemnly. "You'd never believe how terrible it is. First they make you carry heavy stones all night long, and then they pay you for it by beating you until your bones are all jelly!"

And he returned to his woodcutting, and was never lazy again.

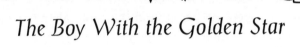

The Boy With the Golden Star

THERE ONCE LIVED a kind and industrious man who had a wife as pretty as a rose. They were happy together, and their only grief was that they had no child.

Every day guests stopped at their house—some of them travelers from faraway countries. They were always welcomed with a smile and made comfortable by their hospitable host. His wife worked all day long cooking delicious meals.

But it so happened that this hospitable house was once left a whole day without a single guest. The man stood in the road in case some stranger might pass by whom he could ask in. He was nearly heartbroken to see night falling without a sign of a guest coming.

He was peering into the darkness for the last time, just before turning back to the house, when he saw an old man, with a white beard down to his waist, coming slowly toward him.

"Good evening, my son," said the old man.

"Welcome, welcome, Grandfather! It is very late to be traveling. If you are not in a hurry, would you care to spend the night in my house?"

"Thank you, my son," said the old man, and he walked after his host with a glad heart. When the young wife saw him her face brightened and she hastened to prepare the best supper she had ever cooked.

As they were sitting around the table after the meal the old man turned to his hosts.

"Tell me," he said, "how is life with you? Have you everything you want?"

"We are very fortunate," said the young wife. "We have all we need. The only thing we miss is a baby to coo in the cradle."

"Then you shall have one," said the old man. "And now, if you will allow me, I must go to bed, for the night is half over and I must be on my way before dawn."

Early the next morning the host accompanied the old man to the end of the village. As they were about to part the old man took a red apple from his pocket and handed it to his host.

"Take this apple home with you and cut it in half," he said. "If you share one of the halves with your wife she will give birth, after nine months, to a bonny baby with a golden star on his forehead. That boy will be braver than all other brave men in the world."

Then the old man searched in his bag and took out a steel sword.

"Take this sword, too," he said. "Keep it carefully and give it to your boy when he grows up. And tell him that he alone is to draw it from its sheath. If someone else's hand draws it, your son will die.

"Now, as for the other half of the apple, you must cut

it in two and give a piece to each of your two fillies. Each will have a foal; one a foal like any other, one a unicorn. You must look after that foal well, because that is the horse your son will ride. And now farewell, I must be on my way."

When the hospitable man arrived home he did exactly as the old man had told him; and not long afterward a boy with a golden star on his forehead was born to his wife, and two foals, one of them a unicorn, to the two fillies.

The boy grew up strong and skillful. He loved hunting and he never failed to catch some gazelles and stags— alive at that. Once he even brought home a bear.

When he was just fifteen the boy heard rumors in the village that in a nearby town there was a man of such great strength that he could break two horseshoes at once.

He went to his father and said, "Father, may I go and try my strength against this man's?"

"Yes, my son, but before you go choose for yourself one of the two horses tethered in the stable," said his father.

The boy went into the stable, grabbed the tail of the horse that had no horn, swung the animal over his head, and threw it outside. Then he took the unicorn by its tail and tried to throw it over as well. But the unicorn did not budge; it stood as if nailed to the ground.

"This is the one for me!" said the boy. He leaped onto its back and rode up to his parents to say good-bye.

The father was delighted when he saw that his son had chosen the unicorn.

"Now you must have the sword that I have been keeping for you," he said. He brought out the sword and gave it to the boy, telling him what the old man had said and warning him earnestly never to let it out of his hands.

Then his mother plucked from the garden two red roses and handed them to her son.

"Keep them well," she said. "They will not fade until you die."

The brave boy thanked his parents and took the gifts. He kissed his mother's hand, and then his father's, and rode away to the town where the famous horseshoe breaker lived. He found the man working in a forge.

"I have heard tales of your strength," said the boy. "Let us see which of us is the stronger."

The blacksmith roared with laughter at the boy's impudence, and good-naturedly agreed to a contest. He snatched up two newly made horseshoes and broke them in half as easily as if they had been two biscuits.

But the young boy stretched out a hand and took three newly made horseshoes. He put them one on top of the other and broke them without the slightest effort.

"You are certainly stronger than I am," said the blacksmith amazed, and bowed low.

Now that he had beaten the blacksmith the boy was eager to try his strength further afield. He spurred on the unicorn and rode off in search of other men famed for their strength. He traveled far and wide until at last he heard of a man whom nobody could overpower. He was said to be as black as soot, and he lived on a faraway mountain.

And so the boy with the golden star rode toward the faraway mountain. As he drew near, a black man appeared from a stone fortress, riding on a pitch-black horse. He galloped furiously toward the boy and shouted from afar, "What are you doing here in my domain?"

The boy with the golden star drew his sword and brandished it in the air. As he swung it, it hissed. The black rider stopped, amazed. He glanced at the sword, then at the unicorn's horn, and quickly jumped down and fell on his knees before the boy.

"Noble rider!" he cried. "I know that neither I nor anyone is stronger than you! From now on I will do anything you ask, if you will only spare my life!"

The boy with the golden star put the sword back in its sheath and dismounted. He followed the black man into the stone fortress, where servants bustled about preparing a rich banquet. They ate and drank and made merry, and when they were mellow with wine they decided to become blood brothers. Then the host started bragging.

"I can turn into anything I like," he boasted. "I can be a bear or a sheep or a donkey, if I feel like it. I can walk on my hands, and when I stand on my head I can pick grapes or pears with my feet."

"That's nothing. What else can you do?"

"When I put my ear to the ground I can hear people talking anywhere in the world."

"That must be useful!" said the boy. He rose from the table. "And now, brother, I must leave you. Good-bye for the present."

"Good-bye, brother, and farewell! When shall I see you again? And how shall I know if everything is well with you?"

"I'll tell you how," said the boy. "Here is a red rose from my mother's garden. She planted a rose tree there the day I was born. It has borne only two buds, but they have bloomed without fading ever since they opened, and they will never fade until the day I die. You take one flower and I will take the other. Look at it every day. So long as it is red, you will know that I am alive."

And then the boy with the golden star mounted the unicorn and galloped away with the swiftness of an eagle. He rode over green meadows and through thick pine forests. He crossed nine rivers. And at every crossroads he asked everyone he met whether they knew of a man braver than all other men. Nobody could tell him of anyone like that.

At last he came to the shore of a deep lake. As he drew near the water to give the unicorn a drink, a man with an enormous stomach ran out of a hut that stood nearby.

"Hey! Don't drink my water!" he shouted. "I have been eating salt fish and I am dying of thirst. I have been waiting for a whole week for the river to fill the lake so that I can have a proper drink."

And the man knelt down there and then at the water's edge and with one gulp emptied the whole lake.

The boy with the star was truly astonished. He dismounted so that he could talk to the man. Before long they were friends, and swore to be blood brothers. When the boy left he gave the second rose to his friend, told him how to understand its message, shook him by the hand, and rode away.

After the boy had journeyed another three months, the unicorn led him one day down into a deep valley. In the middle of the valley stood a tall tower with a roof of golden tiles, encircled by a high wall.

"There must be a rich landlord living here!" thought the boy, and he rode up to a great iron door in the wall.

He knocked once, twice, three times. There was no answer, and the door was locked. The boy, curious to know what was inside, scrambled up the wall and peered over the top. At that very moment a girl of great beauty, dressed in silks, with precious stones glittering on her fingers, came running down the stone steps that led from the tower, and opened the iron door. When she saw the boy with the golden star standing there, her eyes filled with tears.

"Why are you crying, fair lady?" asked the boy.

"I was captured by a cruel robber, who made me his wife against my will," said the girl. "But I am a Czar's daughter, and a year ago I was to be married to a handsome young man like you. On the very day of my wedding, the robber attacked my father's palace and dragged me out of the arms of my bridegroom, whom he killed. I was brought to this lonely place, and here I sit and weep. The days are black for me, even when the sun shines. But now I weep not for myself but for you. To think that you must die, so young and handsome! The robber could kill thousands of men like you!"

"Don't be afraid," said the boy with the golden star, "I'll soon send him into another world."

The robber had been hunting that day. As he was riding home he saw, from a long way off, his wife talking to a horseman. Fury shook him. He spurred his horse and galloped forward, sparks flying from under his horse's hoofs. But as he rode up to the door the boy with the golden star drew out his sword with a flourish. With a single blow he sliced the robber's horse in two, and as the robber fell to the ground he flashed his sword again and killed him.

The beautiful girl stood watching. She had snatched up a long knife, for she was ready to kill herself if the robber won the fight. But as soon as she saw that he was dead she flung away her knife and ran to embrace the victor, with tears in her eyes.

After that, of course, as soon as the young man had put the unicorn in the stable, they were married. And they lived together very happily in the tower.

All this eventually reached the ears of the Czar himself. When he heard that the robber was dead, he sent word to his daughter ordering her to return and marry a neighboring prince.

"Tell my father," said the girl to the envoys, "that I am already married."

The Czar was very angry when he heard the news. He

wanted to find somebody to kill his new son-in-law, but nobody would do it. Then one day a witch as cunning as a fox arrived at his palace.

"I am ready to kill the young man, Your Majesty, and bring your daughter back," she said. "Will you reward me well?"

"I will give you a bag of golden coins," promised the Czar.

The witch dressed herself as a beggar woman and went straight to the tower where the boy with the golden star lived. He was out hunting that day, and it was his young wife who came to see who was knocking at the door.

"Have pity on me, young woman!" said the witch. "I have not a crumb of bread left at home. Give me something to eat, I beg you!"

The girl had a soft heart. She brought out a basket full of bread and roast meat and fruit, and, handing it to the witch, said, "Come back when you need some more. I am often alone here. We'll have a chat and I'll give you something to take home with you."

The next day, as soon as the young man had gone out hunting, the witch knocked on the door again. And that day, the next day, and the day after that she talked to the Czar's daughter, till she was friendly with the girl. Once the old woman asked her if she enjoyed life with her husband.

"We are happy together. My husband has no secrets from me," said the girl.

"You mustn't believe what a man says too easily," said

the witch. "Your husband has his own secrets, I'm sure. Just try to find out what they are. Ask him where the secret of his life lies, and you'll find that he will not tell you."

"Oh, he will certainly tell me!" cried the girl.

The witch went away chuckling to herself. That evening when the young bride had laid the table, she sat silently in a corner. She was not feeling gay.

"Why are you so sad?" asked her husband.

"You haven't any secrets from me, have you?" said the girl.

"Of course I haven't!"

"Then why haven't you told me where the secret of your life is hidden?"

"Oh," said the young man. "I can't do that. Something dreadful might happen if I told anybody."

"Oh, please tell me!" begged the girl, her eyes filling with tears. "It can't matter just to tell your wife!"

"Don't cry—I'll tell you if you really want to know," said the young man hastily, and he gave her a kiss. "The secret of my life is in this sword hanging at my waist. As long as I draw the sword myself, I shall be all right. But if anyone else draws it from the sheath, I shall die at once.

"That is my secret, but you must promise never to tell it to anyone else, or I shall surely die."

But the Czar's daughter could not keep a secret, and the next day the witch heard all about it.

This was the chance the witch had been waiting for.

When evening came she said good-bye to the girl as usual, but once outside she miaowed three times and was instantly changed into a cat. In this disguise she sneaked in again under the door and crept upstairs to hide under the young man's bed.

When the young man came in he took off his sword and hung it carefully on the wall. As soon as he was asleep the cat crept out from under the bed and changed herself back into an old woman. Seizing the sword, she drew it out of its sheath and flung it out of the window into the lake below. And at that very moment the young man stopped breathing.

The witch ran straight to the Czar's palace to tell him his son-in-law was dead, and the Czar at once ordered a regiment of soldiers to go and fetch his daughter back. But when they arrived at the tower the unicorn ran out and attacked them. Rearing up on his hind legs, he pounded the soldiers' heads with his front hoofs; and not a single soldier did he allow to approach the iron door or the girl who was weeping inside.

Now, the very moment that the boy with the golden star had stopped breathing, the red roses that he had given his two blood brothers withered and died. And seeing this, each thought to himself, "My blood brother is dead!" and resolved to find out what had happened to him.

Now luckily the man with the big stomach had heard all about the black man from the boy with the golden star, so he leaped onto the back of a mountain eagle and urged it swiftly toward the fortress, thinking that the black man might know something. When he arrived he found the black man kneeling with his ear pressed to the ground. He was listening to the witch talking to the Czar.

"No sooner had I drawn the sword than he stopped breathing," she was saying.

"And where is the sword?" asked the Czar.

"I threw it into the lake behind the tower."

"Aha!" cried the black man. "The old witch has killed him!"

"Then let us go and bring him back to life," said the man with the huge stomach. And when he had explained who he was he climbed onto the eagle's back again, and the other blood brother mounted another eagle, and they flew together toward the tower.

The eagles swooped down to the shores of the lake, and the man with the big stomach bent down and drank up all the water in one huge gulp. There at the bottom of the lake lay the glittering sword.

The first blood brother snatched up the sword and rushed into the tower and up the stairs to the bedroom where the young man lay dead. He slid the sword back into its sheath, and that same instant the young man rubbed his eyes and rose from the bed.

Outside he could hear the sound of battle, for the unicorn was still fighting the Czar's soldiers. He took his sword and ran downstairs. As soon as the soldiers heard the sharp sword swishing over their heads, they took to their heels and ran away like frightened chickens.

Then the boy with the golden star embraced his wife

and thanked his blood brothers heartily for rescuing him. He sent for his old parents and ordered a great celebration. But before the banqueting and merrymaking began he fetched the old witch from her hovel and tied her up in a sack with some heavy stones. The lake had filled up to the brim again. And when the young man cast the sack into the water it sank to the very bottom, and the witch was never seen again.

ABOUT THE AUTHOR

RADOST PRIDHAM believes that one of the best ways to approach learning about a country is through the legends and folklore of its people. However, she also has firsthand knowledge of Bulgaria since she was raised and educated in Sofia, Bulgaria's capital. Born in Washington, D. C., Mrs. Pridham traveled to the Balkans at an early age. When she was sixteen years old, she began to write short stories and articles which were published in Bulgarian newspapers and journals, and eventually she became editor of a Bulgarian women's magazine. Later, Mrs. Pridham went to England where she and her husband, a retired army officer, are now living. Mrs. Pridham lists her interests as politics and journalism, and her hobbies as reading and talking with people.